IN
PURSUIT
OF THE
PAINTER

In Pursuit of the Painter

ASHTYN NEWBOLD

THREE LEAF
PUBLISHING

ISBN: 9798475997123

Cover design by Ashtyn Newbold

Three Leaf Publishing, LLC

www.ashtynnewbold.com

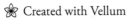 Created with Vellum

CHAPTER ONE

Spring, 1816

Beautiful was the sight of Briarwood in spring, with its lush green grounds, bright stone, and symmetrical wings. But even more beautiful was the sight of its owner, Lord Ryecombe, being struck squarely in the mouth by a cricket ball.

Michael Cavinder wiped a bead of sweat from his brow as he watched the ordeal from afar. The field where they played their cricket match was packed with much more capable men than himself, so he didn't feel the need to rush to Lord Ryecombe's aid. In fact, his friend and teammate, Dr. Cooper, was already running to the man's side, though Michael doubted the earl's pride would allow any assistance.

As Michael surveyed the field, he found that the spectators that gathered on the side consisting of ladies and gentlemen looked on with concern, while those gathered to watch the working class team barely managed to disguise their amusement. If this were the Roman Colosseum, they might have even been cheering. It was not, however, such a riotous affair as that. Lord Ryecombe would never have allowed anything uncivilized to occur on his property, after all—unless he counted his own injustices toward those beneath his station. No, indeed, this was an organized and proper cricket match.

One that had just taken a very entertaining turn.

Walking closer, Michael adjusted his sleeve that had begun unrolling. Shielding his gaze from the sun with one hand, he watched Lord Ryecombe rock back and forth, one hand pressed against his mouth. He was sputtering various demands, his grating voice hindered by his injury.

"Continue with the match!"

Dr. Cooper continued his attempts to assist Lord Ryecombe, who was behaving quite like an angry bee. Michael had always admired doctors. They seemed to possess a patience and goodness that most others lacked. Dr. Cooper was not the only physician of Michael's acquaintance. He had known two other men, Dr. Owen Kellaway, the physician who had treated his father during his last visit in Surrey, and his cousin, Dr. Luke Pembroke. Both men were just as noble as Dr. Cooper.

The earl shifted away from Dr. Cooper, eyes flashing dangerously. He had more hair than patience, and that was saying a great deal, considering he only had a few sprigs of hair remaining on his head.

The earl growled at Dr. Cooper, his speech hindered once again by his swollen lip. "He'll pay for this!"

The man who had hit the ball in Lord Ryecombe's direction was a man Michael knew to work in the post office, Reginald Sinclair. He didn't seem distressed in the slightest. He held the sturdy bat in one hand, and Michael caught the corner of his mouth lifting in a smirk before it straightened again for the sake of appearances.

It really was a shame. Being hit by a cricket ball was not an enjoyable experience, but neither was living days on end with very little to eat because a greedy earl would not pay for the portrait he had commissioned. Because the earl had delayed his payment for the portrait Michael's father had painted—a sum their family had desperately needed—they had been unable to afford *both* adequate food and the rent of his father's shop. They had chosen the rent.

Michael cleared his throat, waiting eagerly for the game to resume. He would take great pleasure in winning against Lord Ryecombe's team. It wasn't that Michael disliked *all* gentlemen—only the ones who gave themselves airs.

It didn't take long before Lord Ryecombe removed himself from the field and the game resumed. The earl observed the game from the edge of the field with a rag held to his lip, his thick side whiskers framing his watchful expression. Each time a point was scored for his team, his triumphant bellows were enough to push Michael to play even harder. Sweat poured from Michael's hairline as the sun beat down upon them. It had been raining for weeks—why couldn't it have at least been cloudy that day? Painting was not often a physically taxing occupation, aside from climbing ladders and holding palettes or his own arm upright for long periods of time, yet he found himself running faster than many of the gentlemen. Michael's team was stronger, and that showed as the game progressed.

He looked out at the crowd observing the game from Lord Ryecombe's side. His gaze caught on one group of young ladies in particular. They giggled and whispered as they watched the match, their pastel dresses and lace parasols uniting them much like the team of gentlemen in their expensive white cricket uniforms.

One lady though, standing just to the right of the giggling group, seemed intent to set herself apart from the crowd. She wore a deep blue pelisse despite the heat. The many intricate pleats and gathers in the thick fabric seemed to be the cause of her stiff posture. Or perhaps it was just in her nature to stand like a board was against her back. The many frills from her chemisette climbed her long neck, encircling her chin. Her hat matched her pelisse, adorned with feathers. The parasol she held over her shoulder shaded her pale skin from the sunlight as she cast a keen eye about the field, her dark brows drawn together.

Michael might not have known the terms for all her feminine accessories if not for his younger sister and her dreams of wearing such finery. He was distracted by the young woman for long enough to nearly lose a point to the opposing team. It wasn't her ridiculous clothing or even her pretty face that had him so distracted. It was the fact that she was staring at him.

Most ladies came to watch the gentlemen team play, did they not? What interest would the women on that side of the field have in his team?

He glanced at the group of giggling ladies again. They were watching Michael and his teammates with expressions he could only describe as ogling. He suspected that they were secretly cheering for them, though they would never have expressed it in the riotous cheers of the opposite side of the field.

As the game continued, Michael ignored Lord Ryecombe's obnoxious shouting, but it was much more difficult to ignore the young woman in the blue pelisse. Each time he glanced her way, her gaze was still fixed on him. Her face showed no amusement, nor emotion. Her back remained rigid, her nose upturned. She might have been a statue if her gloved fingers hadn't been tapping against the handle of her parasol. Were his cricket abilities truly so captivating? He *was* playing better than he ever had before. He was unaccustomed to attention from ladies dressed in fine fabrics and feathered hats. He scarcely knew what to make of it.

Focus. Michael turned his attention back to the game just as his teammate scored the winning point. Lord Ryecombe's disgruntled shout of defeat was everything Michael had been hoping for. He grinned as his teammates walked humbly to their families, who cheered loud enough to make Michael's ears ring.

He wiped the perspiration from his forehead, smiling broadly as his friend Edward Steele approached from the side of the field. He and Michael had been friends for years. Edward hadn't played in the match, but as a talented wood-carver, he had carved the bats they had used during the game. The two had become friends over their shared love of the arts—painting and carving. But they also shared a special dislike of Lord Ryecombe. Who didn't?

"Well done with the bats, Steele," Michael said.

"Thank you," Edward returned. "And well done on your victory." He glanced to the disgruntled earl. Lowering his voice, he said, "Did you see who hit the ball at Lord Ryecombe?"

Michael laughed. "Does it matter who did so long as we all got to witness it?"

Edward shook his head in amusement. Michael rubbed his jaw, lowering his voice to match Edward's. "You know, my father painted the earl's portrait. I do wonder if he should make an adjustment to Lord Ryecombe's likeness now that he'll have a proper scar on his lip."

Edward chuckled as Michael passed, tipping his head in departure. Michael needed a drink of water. Or, better yet, lemonade. It was so blasted hot. He looked back at Lord Ryecombe again, distracted by the discussion he was now having with another of Michael's teammates, Philip Jenkins. Philip's irritation was obvious, and not at all surprising. Any conversation with the earl was bound to end in frustration.

Michael's jovial mood persisted as he crossed the field to the refreshment table. He hadn't been so cheerful in a very long time. With his father being ill and the future so uncertain, he hadn't had time or reason to be anything but serious. His father's business would soon be in his hands. Winning the match that day wouldn't change the fact that he still didn't have work and he still didn't have the slightest idea of how he was going to provide for his mother and sisters.

The smile slowly faded from his face, and he scowled down at his cup of lemonade as he drank from it. The tart drink was refreshing, so he gulped down another glass.

"Well done, Cavinder."

He thanked the man who offered his congratulations with a nod. He was the town cordwainer, and the only man in sight who was dressed like Michael. Surrounded by ladies and gentlemen, he felt quite out of place. Taking his cup with him, he began walking back to the other side of the field. Before he could make it three steps, however, a flash of blue fabric caught his eye.

He turned just as the young lady with the stiff back and intent gaze stepped in front of him. He froze, surprised to find her directly in his path. Surprised, *and* slightly disturbed. How had she found him?

"Did I hear you called Cavinder?" The young woman's voice was more commanding than he had expected, even with her elegant and intimidating appearance. Seeing her at a closer proximity, she was much taller than he had originally thought. Michael was accustomed to towering over most women, but this lady's eyes were almost level with his own. Her arched eyebrows framed a pair of striking hazel eyes, and chestnut brown curls spilled out of her hat.

It took Michael a moment to recover from the shock of her speaking to him. "Yes," he said. "That is my name." He swallowed, glancing right and left. Was she here alone? It didn't seem right that a lady as young and distinguished as she would be at a cricket match with no chaperone. Perhaps she did not need a chaperone because everyone feared her. She had a presence that could take up the entire field, so Michael was surprised that no one seemed to notice that she was addressing him.

"Do you have a relation to Richard Cavinder?" she asked.

He nodded. "He is my father."

"And an artist?"

"Yes." He wiped at his forehead again before adopting a more professional posture. If this seemingly wealthy lady was an interested client, he ought to take advantage of that. "May we be of service to you?"

"We?" One of her dark eyebrows lifted.

"My father is ill and unable to continue with his work. However, I—"

She stopped him by raising one hand, just a small motion of her fingers. "If your father is unable to complete my portrait, then I will seek a different artist."

Michael bit the inside of his cheek, fighting the frustration that rose in his chest. The lady's interest had already faded. She turned, taking one step away from him.

"Miss—" he stepped around her, returning to her line of sight. She didn't appear surprised in the slightest. She let out an airy sigh.

"Patience," she said.

Michael scowled. Why was she telling *him* to be patient? It seemed she was the impatient one, walking away before he could explain himself.

His confusion must have shown. She cleared her throat. "*Lady* Patience. Did you only stop me to inquire after my name?"

Understanding dawned on him. Lady Patience was her name. "No, that is not all." He shook his head. "I see that you have been impressed with my father's work."

"His work is suitable, I suppose. As an artist local to Inglesbatch I daresay he is the best option I have."

Michael tried not to be offended on his father's behalf. Women like Lady Patience were not bred to be complimentary toward those beneath their stations. If her words had not reminded him, her eyes had. As she looked at him, she seemed to be staring at a wet leaf stuck on her boot rather than a human being.

He straightened his posture. "I can assure you, I have been trained by my father my entire life. He studied at the Royal Academy of Arts and has passed his knowledge to me. If you will allow me to complete your portrait in his stead, the quality will be comparable to his work." Michael held his breath. He had yet to take on any real clients of his own, but she did not need to know that. He was ready. He *knew* he was, and his father believed in him too.

Lady Patience studied him up and down, much like one might appraise horseflesh. "He has passed his knowledge to you, but has he passed his talent? If your skill in painting is comparable to how you play cricket, I would think not."

He stood in shock for a short moment. The woman had just insulted him without a single blink of her eyes. Her face didn't even twitch with remorse as she stared at him. He tried to keep his mouth shut, but he couldn't help himself. "I'll have you know, we won the game."

"Your teammate eliminated our best player." She raised her chin. "I think it was done intentionally in an attempt to cheat."

First she insulted him, then accused him of cheating? Michael scoffed. "Your best player? *Lord Ryecombe?* He only played because he's hosting this event." He laughed in his throat. "The team provided greater competition for us once he was off the field and could hinder them no longer. By no man's opinion would Lord Ryecombe be considered the best player on the gentleman's team. A horse with its legs strapped together would play better than he did." It certainly wasn't wise to speak of their host that way, especially to a lady, but Michael had forgotten his place, evidenced by the first sign of emotion he had yet seen on Lady Patience's face.

A line formed on her forehead, right between her eyebrows. "I must disagree."

"I must disagree with you as well, my lady. Politely," Michael added. "I must also politely assure you that my father did indeed pass his talent to me alongside his knowledge. So, would you like a half-length or three-quarter likeness? Miniature or portrait?" He cast a quick prayer through this heart. If she would allow him to paint her portrait, the payment would be at least thirty pounds—enough to rent the shop for a few months as well as provide ample food for his family.

Lady Patience stared at him for a long moment, that crease between her eyebrows deepening. Her gaze flitted to the right. Michael followed her eyes, catching sight of a lady approaching from across the field. Her chaperone, perhaps? Lady Patience's posture seemed to stiffen even more, if that were even possible. She turned her attention back to him, her voice quicker than before. "You are still an apprentice, are you not?"

He took a deep breath. "Yes, however—"

"You must prove that your father has passed his talent to you." Her chin lifted again. "If I do not approve of my portrait, then I will not pay you for it. You must agree to these terms."

Michael's blood boiled. Thirty pounds was nothing to a woman of Lady Patience's standing. She likely carried a greater sum in her smallest reticule. Was this something that all pompous, vain, wealthy people did? Lord Ryecombe had done a similar thing to many people of Michael's acquaintance, including his father when he had painted the earl's portrait. Lord Ryecombe had waited to pay him until the portrait had been admired by his friends. Michael's friend, Edward Steele, likely hadn't even been paid for carving the bats for the cricket match that day.

"Well?" Lady Patience was being quite impatient again. "Do you agree?"

Michael let out a sigh. He was confident that he could prove himself, even if he was vexed by her utter audacity to place such terms on the agreement. "Very well, I agree."

At the words, she took a step back, turning her body partially away from him. He caught sight of three large brass buttons on the back of her blue pelisse. Why on earth would she wear a jacket in this weather?

"I will make my appointment for Monday next at ten o'clock," she said. "A three-quarter portrait."

He gave a quick nod. "So you are aware, the price for such a work is thirty-five pounds."

She smoothed a wrinkle from the edge of her sleeve, the wrinkle in her forehead fading at the same instant. "Only *if* you prove yourself as talented as you claim to be." She took another step away, not offering even a nod in departure.

"You sound much like Lord Ryecombe," he muttered, no longer worried about politeness. He thought he had spoken quietly enough to avoid being heard, but she turned back. Her hazel eyes settled on him, ripe with arrogance.

"As I should. My father has passed his knowledge and talent to me as well."

Michael's stomach clenched as she turned away, hurrying toward the woman who was approaching from the right. They walked across the field without looking back.

Lady Patience was Lord Ryecombe's *daughter*?

And Michael had thoroughly insulted the man right in front of her. He stared at the brass buttons on the back of Lady Patience's pelisse as she walked away. He ought to have been embarrassed or ashamed, but instead, he was amused. A grin pulled on his mouth. It was no wonder Lady Patience was such an unpleasant, pompous woman, unafraid to throw insults and demands at those she deemed beneath her status. As the daughter of an earl, she had wholeheartedly claimed those privileges.

Determination rose in his chest. He would collect her payment. He would not fail his family. He had been practicing for so many years, and there was nothing that could stop him. His father was dying, but Michael would not allow his business to die too. He would make his father proud before his life ran out and he missed what he raised Michael to be.

He glanced at the place he had last seen Lord Ryecombe. The man was lingering by the refreshment table, cringing as he tried to drink lemonade with this swollen lip. Michael tried to recall the man's surname, finally settling on the right answer in his mind. Hansford.

Lady Patience *Hansford.*

That was the name of his very first client.

CHAPTER TWO

*B*y candlelight, the drawing room of Briarwood was showcased at its best. Warm light from the flickering flames bounced between the wooden furnishings and the red velvet chairs, creating a golden glow to the room. That same golden glow settled over Patience's skin and ivory gown, showcasing her at her best as well. This was not a time to be anything but her best, not now that she had finally captured a seat beside Lord Clitheroe.

The marquess had played on her father's team in the cricket match earlier that day, and he had accepted the invitation to return for dinner that evening alongside several other guests. He had never dined at Briarwood before, and he might not ever again, so Patience had to take advantage of this opportunity while it was before her.

"You played well today, my lord." She spoke in the way she had rehearsed during her season in London—coy and confident at once. It was a fine balance. Even with all her practice, she had failed to make a match during her season. She had received several proposals, but none had been a marquess, and that was the problem. She needed, at minimum, an earl, but it was never unwise to aspire to greater heights.

Lord Clitheroe twirled a lock of his hair around one of his fingers as he leaned an elbow on his lap. He cast her a playful smile, his eyes half-closed. "I did not play well enough."

She consoled him with a glance. "Oh, you are too critical of yourself." She lowered her voice. "I do believe the opposing team cheated. How else could they have won?"

Lord Clitheroe smoothed his waistcoat as his posture straightened. "I have the same suspicion. Those men cannot be trusted. They are riotous and uncivilized. I was appalled for your father's sake when he was struck by the ball due to their carelessness."

"My father would be grateful for your sympathy." Patience studied Lord Clitheroe's face. Did he ever open his eyes fully? They seemed to be constantly hooded by his eyelids, and his lips were always curled in a smug grin. He was handsome enough, though not nearly as handsome as half the men on the opposing team had been. If she could have traded Mr. Cavinder's appearance with Lord Clitheroe's then he would be the perfect man. Obviously, this imaginary man would have the marquess's wealth and title. As far as his character was concerned, she would certainly prefer Lord Clitheroe's, for he had not insulted her father as Mr. Cavinder had that day.

"I hope you will forgive my boldness," Lord Clitheroe said, "but I must compliment your gown. I have rarely seen such fine…craftsmanship." His eyes swept over her figure without reservation. Patience resisted the urge to shift away. Her mother had suggested the deeper neckline, reminding her that men fell in love with their eyes first, and if Patience were to secure a marquess, she would have to give him plenty to look at. Her stomach turned when his eyes finally returned to her face.

"I thank you, my lord. All compliments from you will be happily received, I assure you." She offered a flirtatious smile, fluttering her lashes as she looked down at her lap.

"We are in agreement, my lady," he said in his slurred, dramatic voice. "I would happily receive compliments from you just as well."

"Oh?" She looked up, surprised to find him watching her expectantly.

"Have you yet to find something to admire in me?" His smile lifted more on one side, his thick side whiskers hiding a dimple.

"Well—yes, indeed I have." She straightened her shoulders. She caught her mother watching them from across the room, hiding her attentive gaze with a book. The many guests mingled all around her, so she was grateful that her mother would be unable to overhear the conversation. Her mind swirled anxiously as she tried to think of a compliment to offer. "Your cravat…the knot is very intricate. I do quite like an intricately knotted cravat on a man." She grimaced inwardly at her awkward choice of words. She would never be as talented at flirting as her elder sister.

Lord Clitheroe touched a hand to his neckcloth, the other side of his lips rising to complete his grin. "Ah, I am glad that it did not go unnoticed." He smoothed a hand over his hair. "Though I cannot take credit for it. I have the most skilled valet in the entire county, I am sure. It is very important to be presented well in all aspects of life."

Patience nodded her agreement, her back aching from maintaining her stiff posture all evening. Her scalp also ached, sore from holding her heavy hair atop her head.

"Your father showed me the portrait gallery this morning before the match," Lord Clitheroe said in a slow voice. "I did not see your likeness there among the others. I saw your sister, and she is indeed a rare beauty. I now find that beauty has been pronounced upon all the Hansford women."

Patience's stomach twisted as it usually did when she was compared to Hattie, even if it was meant to be complimentary. "My likeness was taken once, but my father disposed of the painting because he did not feel I was properly portrayed." Patience lifted her chin. "He is quite selective when it comes to artists." Patience remembered the long hours of posing for the portrait. Her muscles had been shaking. Her father had hung the portrait for a week and then taken it down because it hadn't compared to Hattie's, not receiving as much praise by his guests. Hattie herself was a work of art, so how could Patience ever hope to compare?

"Who painted his own portrait?" Lord Clitheroe asked. "The artist must have been quite talented to have won his approval."

"Mr. Richard Cavinder."

"Hmm." The marquess rubbed his chin. "I have not heard of him. Perhaps I will have him paint my next. My last is quite outdated now."

Patience shook her head softly. "I'm afraid, my lord, that he is no longer in practice. His son is now working in his stead."

"Is that so?" Lord Clitheroe cocked one eyebrow. "Then that is even more ideal. I have never trusted old men with their feeble hands with the delicate work of painting. The son is likely more robust and capable. I shall trust your opinion and schedule an appointment with him."

Patience swallowed, her nostrils flaring. "Well…the son hasn't yet proven his talent. I would not wish to direct you to his shop without knowing his skill."

"How should we know if we do not try?"

Patience was going to try, that much had been determined earlier that day at the cricket match. Her father had promised a new likeness would be taken of her for her twenty-first birthday, this time by a more talented artist. Perhaps he and her mother hoped that by then Patience's beauty would finally be as notable as her elder sister's. But that was still six months away, and Patience was growing quite, well…*impatient*.

When she had found Mr. Cavinder during the match that day, she had been most eager to speak with him. The elder Mr. Cavinder had painted Patience's father's portrait, and it had been sufficient, even with his very selective tastes in art. She wasn't certain the younger Mr. Cavinder could paint as well as his father, but she was willing to take the risk. She had enough pin money to pay him herself, and she would have the portrait hung to surprise her parents. Her heart stung each time she thought of how she was left out of the portrait gallery simply because the previous work hadn't been good enough.

Or, perhaps, because *she* hadn't been good enough.

The idea scratched at her heart, making it sting all over again.

Lord Clitheroe leaned closer. "What troubles you, my dear?"

The endearment was surprising, but promising. Lord Clitheroe was her opportunity to prove her worth to her family. To stand every bit as admired and esteemed as Hattie. "I am not troubled. I do tend to become lost in thought often." She gave a quiet laugh, casting him another flirtatious glance.

"I long to know what you have been thinking of. Do end my misery at once and tell me." The marquess stared deeply into her eyes, his own still half-closed. Did he think it made him appear more handsome? Charming? Tired, perhaps? It didn't matter what the answer was. All that mattered was that this marquess seemed to be intrigued by her. Did he have marriage on his mind? Likely not, as young as he was. He seemed something of a rake, intent only to woo women, not to marry one.

"My sister is engaged," Patience said. "She is in London now, becoming further acquainted with the family of her betrothed. I have been thinking of my happiness on her behalf, and also of my despair that she will be leaving Briarwood." Despair was not the correct word. *Relief* might have been more accurate. Without Hattie in the house, Patience might finally have the opportunity to be noticed.

"I see." The marquess gave a tight-lipped smile. His entire demeanor changed, and he settled back into his chair. "I did wonder where she was this evening. I hoped to make her acquaintance after seeing her portrait in the gallery."

Patience's face grew hot. Had he only been speaking with her because of his interest in Hattie? Her question was answered as he gave a nod to excuse himself, rising to his feet. "It was a pleasure making your acquaintance, my lady. I'm afraid I must now socialize with the other guests whom I have not met." She watched him flit about the room for a moment before he settled on a seat by the fireplace, where he engaged an older gentleman in conversation.

Patience's lungs deflated, her heart sinking to her toes. Heat climbed to her ears, and she was grateful for the dim light to hide the color. She felt much like a weed that had just been plucked from the earth, cast aside and forgotten in an instant. All her hopes for the marquess crashed down over her shoulders, and she felt nearly crushed by the weight of it.

Her mother's eyes captured hers from across the room, a disapproving pucker on her lips. She mouthed something

Patience could not decipher before drawing an exasperated breath. Patience was relieved to see that her father had not witnessed Lord Clitheroe snubbing her. A marquess, in Papa's opinion, could do no wrong, so the only fault he would find would be in Patience. She could already hear the conversation in the back of her mind. *"Hattie would have kept his interest."* Or *"Hattie would have known the correct subjects of conversation that would not bore him."*

Patience straightened her posture, clenching the muscles in her neck to keep her tears at bay. Her mother's scrutiny continued from across the room as Patience sat alone, avoiding her gaze.

Her heart hammered in her chest as she thought of the portrait that would soon be painted of her. Her stomach twisted with nervousness and excitement at once. The young artist Mr. Cavinder had a lofty task ahead of him. It took a great deal to impress her father.

And in turn, it took a great deal to impress *her*.

CHAPTER THREE

*M*ichael could hardly believe his luck. His mother stood in the corner of the kitchen in their small apartment, her eyes as round as the saucers on which she placed two teacups. "The Marquess of Clitheroe? Are you certain it was him?"

"Of course," Michael said with a laugh. "He has requested a portrait from *me* specifically. He is traveling to London soon, but he has already made an appointment for when he returns to Inglesbatch next month." He drew a deep breath, suddenly nervous and overwhelmed. Was he prepared to paint a portrait for a marquess? Surprisingly enough, he was less nervous about portraying the nobleman than he was about portraying Lady Patience.

"This is wonderful, Michael." Mother walked toward him, setting the tea tray on the nearby table. Her eyes shone with tears as she smiled up at him. Strands of grey mixed in with her dark curls, a contrast that he wished he could portray in his artwork and still have it be admired. If he were entirely realistic, he would have no clients at all. He had been taught that art was meant only to portray beauty and ideals, not signs of realistic aging. Mother squeezed his hand. "I knew you would make us proud."

A surge of emotion flooded his chest, causing fresh determination to rise inside him. "From what I have heard, Lord Clitheroe is an agreeable man. For the gentry," he added. "He seems far more agreeable than Lord Ryecombe, that is for certain." *And his daughter.* Michael cleared his throat, returning to the subject at hand. "What I mean to say is that if he approves of my work, he will be likely to recommend me to his peers. We shall have more business than we know what to do with."

A broad smile pulled on Mother's cheeks. Michael had not seen her smile in a very long time—not since his father's health had begun declining. "You must tell your father," she said. "He will be very pleased to hear it. It will provide him with a measure of peace as well to know that you are able to care for us when he is gone."

Michael removed his hat, raking a hand over his hair. His smile refused to falter from his cheeks. "I will go speak to him now," he said in an eager voice. "Where is Emma? Isabel?" His two sisters were twins, and they could often be found with their arms linked, walking through town and sharing every bit of gossip they had recently heard, or staring at the dresses and accessories in the shops that they could not afford.

His mother gave a soft smile, walking back to the kitchen. "They are reading to Father."

Michael looked toward the narrow stairs that led to the upper bedrooms. He would need the help of his sisters to get the shop presentable in time for his appointment with Lady Patience the following Monday. With so few clients, it had been neglected. He couldn't presently afford new furnishings, but they could clean and organize that which they already had. He was also desperate to speak with his father for any words of advice he might have. Michael's insides turned and flipped.

No, he could not be nervous already.

He still had days to prepare. However, there was one issue that had been troubling him.

"I looked through Father's studio and found his supplies to be lacking." Michael shifted on his feet, looking down at the floorboards. "I must present myself as a professional. The brushes are in adequate condition. As are the paints." He paused. "But there is not even enough canvas remaining in the studio to make one portrait. We have been delaying the purchase of more because we haven't had a need for it until now."

Mother stopped near the pot of stew she had been stirring. Her lips pressed together and her eyes narrowed in thought. "I don't suppose we can afford a new roll of canvas at the moment."

"That is my worry." Michael remembered the long days with little to eat all too well. His stomach was already growling as the smell of beef, potatoes, carrots, and freshly baked bread wafted up to his nose from the kitchen. "Lady Patience requested a three-quarter, so all I will need is a narrow roll. If I purchase one in sixteen ells, it will provide me with enough cloth to make at least twenty-two three quarter portraits. That is far more than I need. I cannot assume even my connection to Lord Clitheroe will provide me with so many clients."

"I believe you can do anything, Michael." Mother's eyes flooded with determination. She reached for the pendant at her neck, unclasping it from the back. "Here." She strode toward him and thrust the necklace into his palm. "Take this to town and sell it. Purchase your roll of canvas, and then purchase another in a greater width. I am certain you will have an abundance of clients."

Michael shook his head, attempting to return the necklace to her. But Mother stopped his hand, closing his fingers around the chain and the glittering pendant that hung from it.

"Mother, I can't sell this." He continued shaking his head. His throat grew tight with emotion. "Father gave it to you."

The determination in her eyes faded for a brief moment, replaced with an expression of wistful longing. "He will be proud to hear that it is being put to good use. The welfare of our family is more important to me than a necklace. This is the only thing of value we have to sell."

He searched her face for any sign of hesitation. Her time with her husband was limited. Michael's father would soon die, and this necklace was something she had to remember him by. "You must keep the one gift Father has given you," Michael said.

Her voice took on a firmer tone, her hand shaking around his. "Your father has given me many gifts that are not material like this. He has given me the happiest of memories. He has taught me what it means to be loved deeply and truly. Those are priceless gifts that I will cherish forever."

Michael was still shaking his head.

"Good heavens, *take it*." Mother's eyes shone with tears. "Take it, and make us both proud." Her hand pulled away from his and she turned toward the pot she had been stirring.

He stood in stunned silence for several seconds, clutching the pendant so tightly that it dug into his palm. Could he do this? The pressure to create a satisfactory portrait was now even more daunting. As his fear increased, so did his courage and determination.

The scent of stew warmed his chest as he walked toward the stairs. He changed his course to Mother's direction, wrapping one arm around her shoulders and giving her a soft squeeze. "Thank you for believing in me. I love you."

She seemed surprised by his affection, for he did not often show it. She patted his hand where it wrapped around her shoulder. "If this is an attempt to earn an extra serving of stew tonight," her eyes shot up to his with half-hearted scrutiny, "it is working."

He laughed, moving to the staircase. "You have discovered my scheme. I will try to be more subtle in the future."

He threw her a wink, to which Mother wagged a finger at him.

Taking the stairs two at a time, he made his way to Father's room, slipping the necklace into his pocket. He stopped by the door, listening to Emma's soft voice as she read aloud. The words were muffled, but the rhythm of her voice told him that she was indeed reading from a book. He pushed open the door as quietly as he could.

Emma looked up from the pages. She sat in a wooden chair by Father's bed, Isabel beside her. He was impressed with himself for recognizing the voice as Emma's. The only way he had learned to tell their voices apart was that Emma's was slightly higher. As for their appearances, Isabel parted her walnut brown hair on the right, and Emma's was parted on the left. Both sets of identical brown eyes met Michael's as he walked farther into the room.

At first glance, Father appeared to be sleeping. His eyes were closed, his hands clasped and resting above the blankets. But the moment Emma stopped reading, Father's eyes fluttered open. "You mustn't stop at the best part of the story. Read on, unless you wish to torture my curiosity."

"What is reading for if not to torture one's curiosity?" Michael said with a grin. "That is the best part of the experience, is it not?"

Father's eyes flickered in Michael's direction. "No, indeed. The best part is indulging it."

Emma smiled down at their father. "Oh, Papa. Wouldn't you rather see Michael for a moment?"

Father's voice was rasped as he turned his head to face

Michael. "Only if he has something more interesting to say than what is written on the pages of that book."

He didn't need to smile for Michael to know he was teasing. The glint in his half-closed eyes was evidence enough. "I think you *might* deem my news worthy of distraction from your book."

Father groaned as he rolled to one side, facing Michael fully. His eyes widened when he saw the smile on Michael's face. "I see it is good news? Indulge my curiosity at once."

Michael took a deep breath. "I have procured two clients for portraits, both of high birth and social standing. Lady Patience Hansford, the daughter of Lord Ryecombe, as well as the Marquess of Clitheroe."

Father propped himself up on one arm, his mouth rounding in gleeful surprise. "You cannot be serious."

"You know I would not lie to you." Pride soared in Michael's chest. "We have stumbled upon a bit of luck this week. I do not know what I have done to deserve it."

"You have been a good man. That is what you have done." Father coughed into the blanket before looking up again with watery eyes. "Do not doubt yourself. Remember all I have taught you and you will create two masterpieces."

Michael's nerves began to relax, and he clasped Father's hand between both of his. "I hope my talent is enough." He turned toward Emma and Isabel. "I will need help from both of you."

"We are not skilled artists," Isabel said. "Papa gave all his skill to you."

Michael shook his head. "There is a skill I lack that you two possess."

"What is it?" Emma asked, leaning forward on her chair.

"I need your help preparing the shop. It must be pretty and presentable for an elegant...and rather captious lady." Lady Patience would be looking for fault in both his work and his service. So he intended to give her nothing to find fault with.

Emma and Isabel nodded, excitement gleaming in their eyes. He hadn't told them yet, but he planned to purchase ballgowns for both of them as soon as he had enough money saved. They would be turning sixteen soon, and he knew how they longed to come out in society and attend a dance.

Michael's heart swelled with gratitude. "Let us start our work today, then."

The first thing he would do was walk to town to sell Mother's necklace and purchase the rolls of canvas. His heart still ached at the thought of Mother's sacrifice, but her belief in him, as well as his father's, gave him strength.

CHAPTER FOUR

"*B*last the rain," Patience muttered as she raced from her coach to the front door of Mr. Cavinder's shop. It had been pouring all day, but there was nothing that could stop her from arriving on time to her appointment. She had worn her finest gown, but even from the ten steps she had taken to reach the front door, the detailed mauve hem had been splashed with dirty water.

She crashed through the door. It chimed when she entered. Pushing it closed behind her, she stopped, gripping the door handle as she caught her breath. Fat droplets of water cascaded down the glass. She wiped gingerly at her cheek, hoping the rouge had not rubbed off with the rain drops. Her hat had only kept some of the water from touching her hair and skin.

"Lady Patience."

The deep voice made her jump. She gathered her

composure, rolling her shoulders back and straightening her spine before turning toward the voice.

As expected, the voice belonged to Mr. Cavinder. He stood near the back of the studio, a tray of paint laid across his muscular forearms. His sleeves were rolled to his elbows, much like they had been during the cricket match. When he lowered his head in a bow, a few strands of his dark brown hair fell over his forehead. Was he scrutinizing her? Was he surprised that she had come without a companion?

She lowered her own head in greeting, allowing her chin to lower just an inch. "Mr. Cavinder."

He strode closer, setting his supplies down on a nearby stool. It was then that Patience noticed two young women standing in the opposite corner of the shop. Her eyes darted between the two faces. They were identical. One girl wore a lavender dress, and the other wore white. That was the only difference Patience could decipher between their appearances.

"Do come in, my lady, and meet my two sisters, Isabel and Emma." Mr. Cavinder brushed his hands off on his trousers, taking another step closer. "They are here to help make you comfortable."

Patience clasped her hands in front of her, interlocking her gloved fingers. She turned toward the two girls, tipping her head in greeting. In response, they walked toward her, offering simultaneous curtsies. Even their brunette ringlets seemed to bounce in unison. "It is an honor to make your acquaintance, Lady Patience," the girl dressed in lavender said. "I am Isabel." She offered a warm smile. "Come, have a seat." She gestured toward a stool with a tufted cushion resting on top. Beside it was a table with a pitcher of water as well as a tea tray filled with scones and dried fruit.

Patience sat on the stool, removing her bonnet and handing it to the other girl. Had her name been Emma? Patience could hardly keep them separated in her mind, so similar were their faces. Without missing a second, Isabel held an ornate looking glass in front of Patience's face. "You may adjust your hair as you see fit."

It was a kind way of pointing out that her bonnet had flattened her curls slightly, and the rain had made some of them stick to the sides of her forehead. Patience tried not to appear flustered as she brushed aside the wayward strands. Her maid had spent hours on the arrangement, and now it would never look as immaculate as it once had.

"Do you require assistance?"

"No." Patience hadn't meant to snap at the girl, but her voice cracked like a whip. "No, thank you." When she finished, she waved the looking glass away with a flick of her hand.

Without the two girls standing in front of her, Patience had a clear view of Mr. Cavinder as he approached. He pulled a smaller, less sturdy stool out from behind a nearby table, setting it across from hers. He sat, clasping his hands together in front of him. "There are a few items that are necessary to discuss before we begin. I believe your original request was a three-quarter?"

"Yes."

Mr. Cavinder nodded. "Very well. Do you have any other requests?"

Patience resisted the urge to scratch her neck. The lace of her collar was dreadfully irritating. "In your depiction, if you must alter any of my features to make them more beautiful, you may do so. That is to say, without losing its likeness to my true appearance. Artists paint according to ideals, do they not? You will not depict my blemishes?" She hoped her nervousness wasn't displayed in her voice.

Mr. Cavinder's gaze lingered on her face, a hint of confusion on his brow. "It would not be a likeness at all if it weren't beautiful, my lady. I assure you, there will be no alterations necessary." He cleared his throat, looking down at the pad of paper in his hand. He held a pencil as well, though he hadn't yet used it to take notes.

His words were quite forward, albeit reassuring. She would excuse them this one time.

"Another matter we must discuss is the amount of time I must ask you to commit to this project," Mr. Cavinder continued. "I estimate that I will require you to pose a total of ten hours, which may be split into three sessions over the next month. The layers of paint will require time to dry between each session."

Patience had fully expected such a time commitment, but it was still daunting to consider. If only she could have the portrait within a week. "Is it possible that the paint could dry with greater speed?"

Mr. Cavinder shook his head slowly. "I am an artist, not a sorcerer."

She scoffed in the back of her throat. "Very well, but is there any *other* way the process could be expedited?"

"The only way could be through shorter sitting sessions, though it could risk the accuracy of the work if the subject is not present for those ten hours." He raised one eyebrow. "The question is, do you live up to your name?"

She scowled before smoothing away the expression. She could not risk acquiring wrinkles. "Pardon me?"

He stood from his stool, marking something on his pad of paper. "A woman with a Christian name such as yours should have no problem waiting," his eyes met hers, "*Patience.*"

"I *am* patient," she said in a defensive voice. She cleared her throat. "I will invest all the time necessary."

Mr. Cavinder's mouth twitched upward. "I am glad to hear it, and I thank you for your cooperation. Should you need anything throughout the process, please inform Miss Emma or Miss Isabel."

Patience nodded, following Mr. Cavinder with her gaze as he moved back to his station. He seemed to have already stretched the canvas over a wooden strainer, though she could only see the corner of it from beyond the easel.

As Mr. Cavinder finished setting up his supplies, she studied him in detail, much like he would soon be studying her. It was only fair that she should inspect him just as thoroughly. His clothing seemed to be second-hand, the threads and seams wearing at the edges, flaws that only a trained eye like hers would notice. His cravat was tied loosely. His face seemed to be freshly shaven, the remnants nothing but a faint shadow on his solid jaw. His eyebrows were dark, like two brushstrokes framing his inquisitive brown eyes.

Though Patience had thought she was an expert in perceiving detail, she realized now that she was a novice compared to Mr. Cavinder. Not only was he trained to recognize the small details of a person, but to replicate them.

"I must apologize," he said suddenly as he moved to stand in front of his easel, "for my words at the cricket match. Had I been aware that Lord Ryecombe was your father, I would not have expressed my opinions so freely."

Patience gave a prim nod. "Your words were quite untoward, indeed, no matter that he was my father." She had not taken personal offense to them, but it had been amusing to see Mr. Cavinder's flustered appearance when she had told him who her father was.

"It does make matters worse though…that he was your father." Mr. Cavinder's eyes met hers as he lifted his pencil to the canvas. "If anyone spoke ill of my father in my presence they would become my swift enemy."

Patience should not have found Mr. Cavinder's conversation so interesting, but if she were to be sitting there for three hours, then she could think of no other way to pass the time. "You are fortunate that I do not make the same rule for myself. You would not want me as your enemy, Mr. Cavinder. I daresay no one would." Patience had been described as intimidating. She couldn't help that she was tall, or that her voice was so direct. She had watched many people cower around her.

Mr. Cavinder raised one eyebrow in curiosity. "Is that so? Have you been known to be vengeful in the past?"

She allowed herself a small smile only after his attention turned to the canvas. "I have not had a reason to be."

"Not even after I said a horse could play cricket better than your father?"

"A horse with its legs strapped together, I believe was the exact phrase. But no, it would require a greater grievance to make me so vengeful."

A smile lifted one half of his mouth. "I am glad to hear it. But again, I offer my apologies." He repositioned the easel, his eyes darting between her and his canvas. When he seemed to decide on a satisfactory position, he walked toward her.

She straightened her spine as he approached. His sharp eyes took her in from head to toe. Though Lord Clitheroe had just done the same at dinner earlier that week, Mr. Cavinder's intentions were different. She felt calm, relaxed...yet somewhat flustered at the same time. Was he taking note of which flaws to omit from the portrait? She tugged on the ends of her long sleeves, keeping them tight against her skin.

"Angle your shoulders more to your right, and tip your chin slightly upward," he instructed.

Patience obeyed, glancing up at him for approval. "Is that enough?"

He nodded before ushering one of his sisters forward. "Adjust the curl on the left side."

The girl followed his directions. "May I?" she asked.

"Yes," Patience said, though she wondered why Mr. Cavinder had not simply done so himself. This was a professional meeting after all. She eyed his hands and forearms. She had never seen such attractive ones in her life. Patience banished the thought, careful not to move her head and shoulders out of position as the girl adjusted a strand of hair on Patience's forehead.

Mr. Cavinder examined her again until he nodded in satisfaction, walking back to his station just a few feet in front of her. "If you grow bored and wish to be entertained," he said, "my sisters will read aloud to you. They have books here on many subjects." His dark brows drew together as he touched the pencil to the canvas. His squared jaw tightened in concentration as he began his work. Good heavens, why couldn't most noblemen be so handsome? Here was a man who did not need elegant clothes and elaborate hair styles to elevate his appearance. In his raw, authentic state, he looked better than them all.

"Is there a certain subject which interests you?" Mr. Cavinder asked.

She shook her head before remembering she was supposed to hold still. "No."

So long as Patience could watch Mr. Cavinder work, there would be no additional entertainment necessary.

"Very well." He seemed amused about something, his lips twitching at the corners. Why was he not intimidated by her? He was far beneath her station and she had threatened not to pay for the portrait if it was not satisfactory. Vexation sprouted in her chest as his subtle smile persisted. She didn't dare ask what it was about. She simply sat still for the hours that followed, until her back and neck ached. The easel was turned away from her, so she couldn't see a single stroke as Mr. Cavinder finished sketching and began painting. She didn't want to see it until it was finished. She was too nervous.

She couldn't understand what exactly made this portrait so important, but at the moment, it was everything to her. It was as if her heart had been crumpled when her father had taken down her first portrait, and the only way to mend it would be to see her likeness on that wall again, proudly displayed beside Hattie's. Perhaps then, and only then, she would not be so invisible.

"That will be all for today," Mr. Cavinder said finally, setting down his brush.

Patience stood immediately, shaking out her numb legs and stretching her back. She had been lost in thought for much of the session, making the time pass faster. Mr. Cavinder's brown eyes were warm and golden, like a fresh cup of translucent coffee. They sparked with mirth. "I thank you for your patience."

"Of course." She looked down at the floor, feeling a sudden urge to look away from those warm brown eyes. They were opened all the way—attentive and inviting, quite unlike Lord Clitheroe's eyes. A scowl pinched at her brow. Was Mr. Cavinder simply being kind because he wanted to win her favor so she would pay him? He must have known what his looks did to women. No matter how far above his station a woman was, she could not rise far enough to mistake the fact that the man was handsome.

It was a shame, really, that he was not a marquess.

She shook herself of her strange thoughts. It would not do to find herself thinking excessively of a painter.

After scheduling her next appointment, Patience gathered her bonnet, leaving the studio—and Mr. Cavinder's inviting eyes—behind her.

At least until the next week.

CHAPTER FIVE

Out the window of Patience's bedchamber, a chorus of birds sang, coaxing the sun over the horizon. Every muscle in Patience's body was tight, even the two fingers that pinched her quill. She wrote to Hattie in her diary sometimes. It was a way to unleash her thoughts and feelings. Hattie would never read those words, but by writing them down, Patience could pretend that Hattie understood how suffocating her shadow had become. She might at least sympathize. She might even defend Patience when their mother belittled her.

Don't be weak, Patience demanded to her heart. Glancing out the window again, she could almost smell the rain-soaked earth. The gray sky beckoned her. She had not risen this early to wallow. Her little ones needed her.

Rising from her desk, she threaded her hair into a braid before covering her bare arms with her soft wool cloak and tugging on a pair of gloves. As quietly as she could, she made her way down the stairs and outside into the rainy morning. This spring had been particularly wet, and it was carrying into the beginning of summer as well. Besides the cricket match, there had hardly been a sunny day in weeks.

Cold water seeped into Patience's boots as she sloshed over the wet lawn where the match had been played. Beyond the manicured field was a row of trees. Patience stopped beneath the second one on the right. It was moments like this that made her glad that she was tall. She only had to rise a few inches on her toes to see inside the nest that was tucked in the attachment site of three branches. The rain had gotten to it, leaving some of the dirt that held the twigs of the nest together muddy. To her relief, the three turquoise, speckled eggs still rested inside, unharmed.

The mother bird swooped down from a nearby branch, and Patience backed away to give her the space she needed. The bird's tiny eyes watched Patience for a minute before it was brave enough to make an inaudible landing on the ground, pecking the wet earth for worms. Patience observed from a distance as the bird took its meal up to the nest, enjoying the fat worm while it warmed the eggs beneath it.

The last time Patience had found a nest filled with eggs on the property, she hadn't had the chance to see them hatch. Her parents had given Hattie a cat for her birthday, just days before Patience expected the eggs to hatch. The next day, when Patience had gone out to check on her nest, that wicked cat had eaten them all. The cat had even eaten the mother bird, evidenced by the feathers on its whiskers and between its claws as it walked away from the scene.

Warm relief cascaded through Patience's chest as she walked away from the tree today. She might just see these babies hatch. Hattie had taken her cat with her to London. So long as she did not return, the birds would be safe.

A trickle of rain had begun falling again, leaving pinpoint dots of moisture on the sleeves of Patience's cloak. It wasn't enough to drive her inside though. These early hours of the morning were hers. She could listen to the chirping of birds, to the rustling of leaves, or to absolutely nothing at all. No demands, no disparaging remarks. Out here by the trees, Patience could slouch her shoulders or spin or watch the birds flying above and wish for the same sort of freedom. And she did wish for it. Every day.

Dread puddled in her stomach like the rain between the protruding roots of the tree. Her family was hosting a soiree that night. Lord Clitheroe would be in attendance, and her mother had been encouraging her to make another attempt at his attention. And somehow she had to sneak away between now and then for her second appointment with the painter.

Mr. Cavinder.

Chills ran up the course of her arms. Surely it was the cold that caused them. Not the thought of the painter. It had been a week since she had last been in his studio, but for an odd reason, she looked forward to going back. The environment was comfortable, and Mr. Cavinder's sisters doted on her. She would not allow herself to add a third reason.

Lord Clitheroe was the only man who could dwell in her thoughts today. She had to plan carefully how she would behave around him, what she would say. She could not afford to ruin this new opportunity. She needed to practice beforehand.

Perhaps she could test a thing or two during her time in Mr. Cavinder's studio that day…an innocent experiment that would put her worries at ease.

Her flirting abilities needed practicing, and she would not mind testing them on a man as handsome as Mr. Cavinder. Not one bit, in fact.

———————⟋⟍⟍———————

Patience Hansford was a peculiar woman. Michael didn't mean to think of her so often, but it was difficult to keep his mind focused on anything else while spending his days working on her portrait. It was strange, but during her first posing session, Michael had felt like the subject. He had never been stared at so intently in his life.

At least, he hadn't been so aware of a stare before.

Lady Patience's eyes were penetrating, sharp, framed in dark curled lashes. The color of her irises had stamped itself in his brain like a hot wax seal, leaving behind strokes of moss green and a golden brown like lightly steeped tea.

To replicate the colors of Lady Patience was a difficult task.

As was properly reflecting her countenance.

One moment, she was condescending and distant. The next, she was attempting to intimidate him. He had caught her in other moments though, when she had seemed to lower her facade just enough to show an exhaustion and defeat behind her gaze. Michael believed people were not often born so stern and serious. There were usually circumstances that made them so.

He didn't thoroughly analyze all of his subjects, but Lady Patience refused to leave his thoughts. His vexation with her was threaded through all his intrigue, leaving a bitter taste in his mouth. Though he wasn't intimidated by her, he was *wary* of her. According to their agreement, she could withhold payment from him for these hours of work if she wished. It was a test, one that Michael should have never agreed to. He hadn't told his family of their agreement, but he already knew his father would have advised him against making it. But he was desperate, and Lady Patience knew it. He was at her mercy.

When the bell above his studio door chimed, he met those hazel eyes with the most polite greeting he could manage. Lady Patience wore the same gown as she had for their first session, the long mauve sleeves ending with lace at her wrists.

"Good day, my lady," Michael said. Emma and Isabel rose from their seats to usher Lady Patience to her stool.

He took to readying his painting supplies. Contrary to

their last two encounters, today Lady Patience seemed intent not to look at him until absolutely necessary. Her attention was focused on the floorboards as Emma and Isabel smoothed the fabric on her shoulders. When their hands moved to smooth and straighten her sleeves, Lady Patience's back stiffened. "I will do that," her voice snapped loud, echoing against the wooden walls. She brought her arms in toward herself, angling her body away from Emma's outstretched hands.

Michael cast a quick warning glance at his sisters, and they backed away from Lady Patience with round eyes. They sat on their chairs in the corner, providing several feet of distance for their client.

Michael observed as Lady Patience tugged the hems of her sleeves into her palms, clamping them down with her fingers. She cleared her throat lightly when she caught him staring, and she pulled her arms even closer to her body. There was a light flush to her cheeks, as though she realized how sudden and impolite her outburst had been. She didn't seem intent to acknowledge it though.

"Would you like to see the portrait as it is thus far?" Michael asked.

A swallow bobbed in Lady Patience's long neck. "No. I will wait until it is finished."

"Are you certain?"

She nodded, her lips pressing together.

"Very well. It will be a surprise." Michael gave a smile that he hoped would calm the nervousness she was exhibiting. Her eyes flitted to his and then fell back to the floor. He sighed. It would not do.

With slow steps, he walked toward her. "May I?"

"May you...?" her dark brows shot up.

"Assist you with your pose."

She hesitated for several seconds before giving a nod so slight he wondered if it had been intentional. Her eyes followed his movements as he slipped his fingers beneath her chin, lifting gently and turning her head at the same angle it had been before. Her skin was velvet under his calloused hands, reminding him of the difference in their stations. His view of her features was better here, standing just a foot away. Each color and line was dramatic, dark, and lovely. Faint freckles dotted her cheeks like stars across a night sky. When her eyes met his, his stomach gave a pathetic flop. *Well, that was uncalled for.* With his other hand, he touched her opposite shoulder, but it did not relax as he had hoped. It only grew more tense. He pressed down softly until the angle was correct.

"There." He turned on his heel, fingertips thrumming with a strange sort of energy. His heart had been jolted by that brief touch, and now it beat just a little differently. How—how on *earth*—had Lord Ryecombe produced such a beautiful daughter? After reaching his sanctuary behind the easel, he met Lady Patience's stoic gaze. "You may request entertainment, food, or drink from my sisters at any time throughout the appointment today."

She was silent for a long moment. "May I request entertainment from *you*?"

Michael hadn't the slightest idea of what to make of her words. "My attention will be a bit occupied." He nodded toward the canvas that faced him.

"Surely you are capable of focusing on more than one thing at once."

He picked up his brush, rolling it between his fingers, already thoroughly distracted. "I'm surprised at your sudden confidence in me. If I am already incapable of painting a suitable portrait of you while being entirely focused, how am I to do so while..." how had she put it? "...entertaining you?" He frowned at the canvas. "Do you wish for me to read while painting? That would be nearly impossible. I could sing, but I assure you, the sound is horrendous."

"You did not mention dancing."

He gave a breathless laugh when he caught sight of her flirtatious smile, extremely concerned with her new behavior toward him. Was she unwell? He cleared his throat. "Of all the things I do not do, dancing is first on the list."

Flirting with the daughter of Lord Ryecombe is second.

He set his jaw, determined to focus on the canvas and not on Lady Patience's distracting smile. He hadn't seen her smile before, but he was fairly certain that now that he had, the image would be etched behind his eyes for the next week.

"Any enjoyment of dancing has much to do with one's partner."

"I imagine that would be true." Michael mixed the color of Lady Patience's eyes on his palette.

"As does one's enjoyment of a conversation rely on the partner."

Michael glanced up just as she pressed her lips together in a coy smile.

"I think I have chosen my partner well today." She watched him with the same intensity she always had, but this time she seemed to be waiting for something. A reaction, perhaps? Despite how bewildered he was, he couldn't give her what she was searching for. Women like Lady Patience must have known the effect their beauty had on men. There was little that rankled Michael as much as vanity. If Michael were daft enough to take her flirtations to heart, he would be a very devastated man when he realized she was toying with him for attention. A man of his station had no place with a woman of hers, and she knew it. Whatever game she was playing, he could play it better.

He didn't miss a step, glancing away from her flirtatious smile with a shrug. "You must be quite easily entertained. I have hardly said a word." His voice was flat as he painted a small stroke across the likeness of Lady Patience's hair.

He heard the air deflate from her lungs in a small *puff*. "What a clever observation. I must now consider that my enjoyment of your company is related to something else entirely." Her voice was filled with false innocence. "What could it be?" She tipped her head to one side, elongating her neck, as if to say, *look at my attractive, smooth skin. You want to touch it. I know you do.*

49

Michael set down his paintbrush, striding straight toward her. A flicker in her strange facade showed her unease, and she licked her lips nervously. This was not the woman who had just flirted two seconds before.

Emma and Isabel were thankfully engaged in a book. He was grateful they were such devoted readers. Nothing short of an earthquake could shake their attention from the pages of their story. He could practically see Lady Patience's pulse racing in her neck as he approached. He reached for her. Her eyes widened.

Furrowing his brow in concentration, he took her chin between his fingertips and returned her head to the correct angle. "Please hold still," he said.

He could practically feel her shocked gaze at his back as he walked to his easel. Had she really feared he would greet her with sudden advances? And with his sisters present no less? At his open and operating business establishment? His amusement deepened and he struggled to hold his laughter at bay. When he turned around again, she was glaring at him.

A frustrated mutter tumbled out of her lips. "If I cannot even attract *your* attention how on earth am I going to attract the attention of a gentleman?"

Ah. That was what this was about, was it? He didn't particularly appreciate being part of her experiment, but luckily he had seen straight through it. Other men would not have been so fortunate. "Er—I will try not to take offense to that. If it is any comfort to your pride, my attention is not easily won, and especially not by such obvious antics as what you just displayed." Gads, he needed to watch his tongue. This woman could walk out of his shop without paying him a shilling if she wished.

Fire shot from her eyes, followed by a resigned sigh. "Advise me, then. What *would* attract your attention?"

He considered her words carefully. He had been so focused on work, art, and his family for years that he had only set his cap on a few young ladies over the years. One daughter of a stone mason, one daughter of the local solicitor. Both had been uninterested in him, and he had soon forgotten them. Neither woman had made a considerable impression on his heart, but he could still recall the prevailing attributes which had attracted him. Humility and kindness.

Michael tried his best to split his attention between his work and Lady Patience's peculiar question. "I assure you, my opinions will likely be different than this gentleman whose attention you are seeking. I am a mere painter." He gave his voice a flare of dramatics, a rare occurrence for him. "What could I possibly know? At any rate, we should not be speaking of these matters."

He thought she would agree with him and return to her prim expression, but instead, deep curiosity burned in her features. "You must tell me. Surely all men are the same in that regard."

He did not like her demanding tone. "In what regard, exactly?"

"In what attracts them to a woman." Her face colored,

as if she were just now recognizing the impropriety of this entire conversation.

"If you are implying that beauty is the only thing that matters, you are wrong." Michael examined Lady Patience's face before completing a stroke of his paintbrush just beneath the likeness of her nose.

Lady Patience's brow twitched in confusion. "That *is* the prevailing theme of poetry."

"If I were to write poetry," Michael said with a smile, "it would likely be intolerable to read, but it would be different. Beauty draws the eye, but it is something else that draws the heart. Something mysterious that has been experienced by many, but is too complex to ever be properly explained."

Lady Patience's frown persisted. "What is it?"

"That is where men vary. What draws my heart is different than what draws the heart of the gentleman you spoke of. If, perchance, he has a heart. I hear some high-and-mighty gentlemen lack that vital organ." He needed to stop. He was about to lose a client and his reputation.

One of her dark eyebrows arched. "Are you referring to my father again?"

"No." Michael was a terrible liar, and that was one reason why he chose to refrain from the practice.

Her eyes narrowed, but she didn't question him. "How am I to know what draws his heart?" She paused. "What draws yours?"

Michael met her gaze with a half-smile. "I thought you might like to know."

Lady Patience's lips sputtered. "Only to apply it to my current situation with the gentleman."

Drat, had he just flirted with her? He hadn't meant to. "Does *the gentleman* have a name?"

"Not one that I would reveal to you. These are *secrets* I'm sharing with you, Mr. Cavinder, and I think I have shared enough already."

"And why have you chosen me to share these secrets with?" He bent closer to the easel, squinting. "You must have a sister or female friend in whom to confide these things, do you not?"

When she didn't respond for several seconds, he glanced up. Her eyes were glazed over, staring at the corner of the room. "No." She clasped her hands before seeming to remember she was supposed to be holding a pose. "I do not."

His brush paused over the canvas.

"I chose you because you are of no consequence to me." Her voice was direct. "As soon as my painting is finished, our paths shall part and we will likely never speak again."

Michael nodded, resuming his work. "It is a wonder then…why we are speaking at all."

Her eyes found his, communicating her agreement without words. They said nothing more for the time that remained of the appointment. Michael worked quickly, careful to avoid those hazel eyes whenever possible. They were deeper than the sea. One moment she was easy to read; the water was clear. The next, it was as if someone had unsettled the bottom of a pond, letting up clouds of mud to obscure that which she kept hidden beneath the surface.

When it came time for her to leave, she replaced her bonnet on her head, turning when she reached the door. "You are surprisingly wise, Mr. Cavinder."

He tipped his head to one side as he removed his smock. "Surprisingly? Again, I will try not to take offense."

Her cheeks twitched, but she didn't quite smile as she stepped outside into the rain.

CHAPTER SIX

"*I* purchased this in town today." Mama's strained voice echoed in the vast corridor near Patience's bedchamber. "I bought it in the hopes that it will elevate your beauty enough to capture Lord Clitheroe's attention."

Patience's chest tightened, her suppressed hope stretching its wings. Mama rarely gave her gifts.

"If that is possible," Mama finished, sending shards of ice over the warmth of her gesture. She walked closer, extending the necklace she had purchased in town. Though Mama was much shorter than Patience, she towered over her in other ways. Patience couldn't help but shrink when she was near. Mama and Hattie looked alike, with their golden curls, large blue eyes, and milky, unblemished skin. Mama had been just as admired as Hattie in her youth, and even at her age now, she had carried her beauty with her.

Patience took the pendant from Mama's hand. It was cold and heavy in her palm. She looked down to examine the piece. It was engraved at the edges, with a pearl embedded at the center. A small piece of lilac amethyst hung by a threadlike chain from the larger pendant. Patience's jaw lowered in surprise.

"It is second-hand," Mama explained. "It did not cost as much as it appears. Lord Clitheroe will not know the difference."

Patience tied the ribbon behind her neck, letting the pendant fall just beneath the notch between her collarbones.

Mama examined it carefully, then circled Patience with a critical eye. "It will have to do." She paused, her eyes catching on Patience's arms. "Half sleeves? These gloves are not long enough. If they shift at all…" her voice trailed off.

"I have longer ones here." Patience walked back into her bedchamber and brought out a different pair of gloves. With a quick tug, she removed the shorter ones and replaced them, face burning. "Is that better?"

"Yes." Mama sighed with relief, rubbing her temple. "You must be more careful in selecting your gowns. If you danced and moved your arms enough to reveal them, Lord Clitheroe would lose interest entirely."

Patience gave a prim nod, biting her tongue. Her heart pounded with dread, and she interlocked her fingers behind her back.

Continuing her examination, Mama's eyes traveled the length of Patience's gown. "Are you taller than the marquess?"

Patience hadn't stood beside him, but he hadn't seemed very tall when she had seen him stand. "I suppose by an inch or two."

Mama's lips pursed, her brows drawing together. "Are you wearing your flattest slippers?"

"Yes."

"Hmm." Mama circled her again. "Perhaps he finds you too masculine. Your features are more like your father's after all." She grimaced, tapping Patience's nose. "And with Hattie joining us at the soiree, I daresay the marquess will be forced to draw comparisons. Hattie, of course, is engaged, but he will still prefer to look at her."

"Hattie is here?" Patience ignored the sinking sensation in her chest.

Mama's lips curled slowly. "Yes, my dear girl has surprised us with a visit. She wished to visit Briarwood one last time alone before she is married."

Patience nodded, gripping the sides of her skirts in her gloved hands. "Even though her wedding is next week? I thought she had a great deal to prepare in London."

"All the preparations are complete now." Mama placed one hand on each of Patience's shoulders, her vibrant blue eyes stabbing through Patience like icicles. "Now all that remains is your wedding. You *will* marry the marquess. Believe it, and it will be so."

Patience swallowed. "Do *you* believe it?"

Mama hesitated. "With effort, I believe it is possible." She patted Patience's shoulder before stepping away. "Be in the drawing room in ten minutes. Do arrive on time."

She glanced back. "Have your maid pinch your cheeks again."

With that, she was gone. Patience released her breath, letting her lungs deflate and reduce the strain on her stays. They had been laced particularly tight that evening. Her entire body felt as though it had been laced tight, and if she made one wrong move, the laces would snap and undo all the efforts Mama had made to impress Lord Clitheroe.

Nine minutes later, Patience walked into the drawing room. The moment her eyes fell on the marquess, her stomach twisted. She tried to recall her conversation with Mr. Cavinder earlier that day. Her practice at flirtation hadn't had the result she had expected, so her confidence was lacking. How should she act? What should she say?

Her gaze turned to the woman she could always count on to demonstrate proper flirting, even when she was engaged to another man.

Hattie stood near Lord Clitheroe, her musical laughter ringing through the room. Golden ringlets framed the arches of her delicate brows and long, curled lashes. Her body leaned toward the marquess as she spoke to him in hushed tones, as though they were sharing a humorous secret. The marquess's attention was already claimed. It was stolen before Patience had even entered the room.

She squared her shoulders when she caught Mama's gaze. Mama gritted her teeth, nodding urgently in the marquess's direction.

Patience hurried forward, stopping just a few paces

behind Hattie. Her legs shook beneath her. Papa had now joined Hattie and the marquess.

"Even more beautiful than her portrait, is she not, Lord Clitheroe?" Papa said.

From where she stood, Patience could only see half of the marquess's face as his eyes perused her sister. "Indeed. That is a rare thing. Often painters depict people in a deceiving manner; in a manner that is too close to perfection to be realistic. But I see now that perfection does indeed exist."

Patience tried to breathe deeply, but her lungs felt as though they had been filled with stones. Would Mr. Cavinder depict her in such a manner that Lord Clitheroe would find her likeness more attractive than her reality? The idea of that was nearly worse than not having a portrait at all. Patience had been compared to Hattie for her entire life, always falling short. To fall short of her own portrait would be devastating.

She stood up taller, finding the courage to approach the trio. She gave a bow in the marquess's direction, stopping between Hattie and her father. Lord Clitheroe's eyes slid over her, a smile curving his lips. "Good evening, my lady."

"Good evening." She tried to replicate the smile she had just seen on Hattie. Demure, subtle, inviting.

"Patience!" Hattie's eyes rounded. "Have you not a greeting for your own sister?" Her tone was accusatory as she flung her arms around Patience's shoulders. "We have been apart for nearly a month, after all." Hattie pulled back to look at her sister. "Have you grown taller?" She laughed. "I didn't think it possible." Her eyes flicked over Patience's entire being in one swoop. "Did you get a new maid? What on earth has she done to your hair? That style was all the rage *last* year." Her voice grew louder as another giggle escaped her. "Perhaps you should share my maid while I am here." She patted Patience on the shoulder much like Mama had in some show of pity.

Patience's cheeks burned as Lord Clitheroe smiled. His eyes followed Hattie as she fluttered across the room to see what other attention she could claim. Patience was fairly certain that her sister could not live without ensuring Patience was beneath her, and insulting her hair arrangement in front of Lord Clitheroe would give her some sort of security. Even when she was engaged, she still couldn't be content without the attention of other men. Patience would have to wait until Hattie was married to have any hope.

When Patience looked up from the floor, Lord Clitheroe was staring at her, eyelids still drooping in that devil-may-care manner. Papa walked away without saying a word, leaving Patience alone with the marquess.

"I have made an appointment with Mr. Cavinder's son," he said. "I look forward to seeing if his work is what you claim it to be."

"I did not—" Patience cleared her throat, offering a shaky smile. "I will not officially recommend him yet."

"Has he completed your portrait?"

"Not yet." Patience glanced about the room to ensure

her father wasn't listening. "I must still visit his studio for a few more hours."

A deep chuckle rumbled from his chest. "I envy the man."

"Why?" Patience leaned closer much like Hattie had done. She tried to slouch just a little, lowering herself the inch or two that separated her height with Lord Clitheroe's. She could not have him thinking she was masculine.

A slow grin climbed his face. "Mr. Cavinder has the privilege of looking upon you for hours without judgment."

Patience froze, stunned by his words. She couldn't think of a reply before he slipped away with a bow and mischievous smile. Hope surged in her chest as she stood alone near the center of the room. She quickly moved to the outskirts, struggling to comprehend the marquess's words. He must have known how forward they were. Any woman would take them as an indication of interest.

To marry a marquess would change her life. She would finally be respected. A future of comfort would be secured for her. She could not ruin this opportunity—especially not now that she had been so encouraged. Lord Clitheroe envied Mr. Cavinder's *privilege*, as he had called it, to look upon her for hours.

Did Mr. Cavinder view it as a privilege? Patience clung to the thought much longer than she should have before letting it sink to the back of her mind where she kept the rest of her uncalled for thoughts about that man.

Throughout the rest of the evening, Patience had

several other opportunities to speak with Lord Clitheroe, most of which were cut short by Hattie's interjections. The marquess couldn't be blamed for being taken with Hattie's beauty, but he knew as well as Patience that she was engaged. His flirtations were better spent on Patience, giving her something to hope for when she retired from the drawing room at the end of the soiree.

She held onto the pendant at her neck as she walked to her bedchamber. Perhaps the necklace was what had given her such luck.

After changing into her night shift, she sat on the edge of her bed. She jumped when the door opened. Hattie walked inside, closing the door behind her. Following closely at her heels was Aphrodite, her long and slender gray cat.

"My dear Patience, I am so happy to be back in Inglesbatch before my wedding. I have missed you."

Patience's shoulders stiffened. The tone of Hattie's voice was stilted—an attempt at sounding genuine. She hadn't come here to tell Patience how much she missed her. There was another hidden reason.

Hattie wandered to the vanity, sitting down in Patience's chair.

"Did you have an enjoyable evening?" Patience asked.

"Indeed." Hattie paused, eyes never leaving her own reflection. "Did you?"

"Yes." Patience swallowed.

Hattie smiled, lifting a comb to her hair. "I couldn't

help but notice that you seemed...flattered by the marquess's attention."

"You mustn't fault me for it. Who wouldn't be just as flattered?"

Hattie pursed her lips. "I don't think Lord Clitheroe is genuine in his flirtations. I would advise you not to set your heart on him."

Patience twisted a loose thread on her night shift. "Why do you think he is not genuine?"

Her sister laughed. "He is a flirt by nature. Besides that, he is a marquess, and you—" Hattie paused, casting her a look of pity. She didn't finish her sentence. Instead, she continued combing her hair in front of the looking glass. Her cat rubbed against her leg at the base of the chair, purring softly when Hattie stroked it between the ears. "Good girl," she cooed to the cat before turning toward Patience. "Isn't Aphrodite the most beautiful cat you have ever seen?"

Patience didn't answer, staring into the cat's bright green eyes. It was a stunning creature, but Patience knew what it was capable of. She met Hattie's eyes in the mirror, round and blue and flooded with false innocence.

What was *she* capable of?

Patience walked to the breakfast room early the next morning. She hadn't been able to sleep well, unease and dread twisting in her stomach and keeping her awake. When she walked inside, she found Hattie already seated at the table. Patience had been looking forward to eating alone before taking her daily walk to the tree to see if the eggs had yet hatched.

At the thought of the birds, she froze, halfway to the sideboard.

"Where is Aphrodite?" She whirled toward Hattie.

She waved a hand passively, taking a dainty bite of bread. "I let her out this morning. Not to worry, she will be safe. She never wanders far and she is very intelligent, you know."

Patience ran from the room, throat tight. Her legs felt heavy as she rushed outside in the light rain, making her way to the tree. She stopped.

Dread pooled in her stomach. It was a memory, that was all.

A memory, she insisted.

A terrible memory.

Tears stung the back of her eyes. As she came closer, she could see that the images were too vivid to be only in her head. Claw marks covered the bark of the tree. A capsized nest. Fragments of vibrant blue eggshells were littered on the ground like a shattered vase.

Aphrodite sauntered out from the cover of the tree, not a single sign of remorse in the creature's gait or expression as it licked its whiskers.

Patience pressed a hand to her heart as tears fell down her cheeks. Not again. The despair in her chest grew as she cried at the base of the tree, the emotion descending into a bitterness so potent it choked her. If she told Hattie what Aphrodite had done, she would tell her that it was silly to cry over three eggs that had never hatched. But Patience couldn't help but mourn with the birds who had been watching over the eggs as eagerly as she had.

The mother bird chirped with confusion as it fluttered around the place where its nest had been, and it broke Patience's heart.

Nothing—*nothing* was safe with Hattie nearby. The sooner Patience learned that, the better. Thick iron gates closed around her chest, surrounding her heart. Nothing was allowed in. Not again. No feelings, no pain, no little birds.

CHAPTER SEVEN

"When paint is spread thin enough and left alone for too long, what do you suppose happens to it?" Michael asked Emma and Isabel.

"It hardens," Emma said.

"Indeed." He scraped at a mistake he had made at the corner of Lady Patience's portrait. "Not only that, but it becomes cruel and unforgiving." After a great deal of coaxing, he managed to remove the hardened lump of paint.

The bell on the studio door chimed, indicating Lady Patience's arrival. She was early today.

Though Michael hadn't seen her in a week, he had been working on her portrait, and by now he seemed to know her hauntingly beautiful features better than his own. He was proud of his work. It was nearly complete.

As she walked through the door, he was reminded that she was far more beautiful in person than she was on the canvas. Would she approve of his work? His stomach flipped as she walked in. Their last conversation had been very odd, and she likely felt the effects of it still lingering between them as much as he did.

"Lady Patience," he greeted with a smile. "I trust you have had an enjoyable week?"

She didn't reply for several seconds as she settled into her stool. Her gaze found his before flickering to the floor. "Yes."

"I am glad to hear it." Michael watched her carefully. Why did he sense she had lied to him?

He began gathering his painting supplies, sending Emma and Isabel to attend to Lady Patience in their routine manner. It was not his business to know, but his curiosity couldn't be helped. "Did your efforts to win over *the gentleman* meet with success?"

"It has only been one week. I could not have won him over already. Not completely."

"Yes, it will take time. High opinions are won little by little. Love, however, is a bit more unpredictable."

"How so?" Lady Patience threw him an incredulous look.

Michael couldn't pretend to be an expert at love, given his inexperience with such matters, but as an artistic person, he had always thought deeply enough and read enough to come to his own conclusions. He tried to clean a bit of dried paint from his brush, but it wouldn't come off. He tossed it to the floor, picking up a clean one to use instead.

"Sometimes love comes gradually, but other times, I

have heard it sneaks up like a thief, set on taking your heart and giving it away without warning." Michael scowled as he contemplated the analogy. "Or perhaps love is not a thief, but rather it returns your heart to the place it has always belonged—with the person you love." He had always enjoyed giving life to inanimate things, such as love. It was what he did with his paintings too—bring life to a boring piece of cloth wrapped around a frame of wood.

Lady Patience stared at him for a long moment before the corner of her lips twitched. "I think you should have been a poet."

Michael laughed. "I confess, I do have the heart of one. But I'm afraid painting is my only useful talent." He glanced up, meeting her gaze before focusing on his work. He was still learning how to do his work correctly, but he assumed that speaking of matters such as love with his female clients would be frowned upon. Especially when he found himself increasingly intrigued by that particular client.

He shook his head. *No.* No. No. No. He refused to be even the slightest bit smitten by a woman so far above his station—and the daughter of Lord Ryecombe, no less. As soon as he finished her portrait, he was confident he would never think of her again.

At least he would *try* not to.

Lady Patience's brow furrowed. "How will I know if *the gentleman* is falling in love with me?" Lady Patience's features turned thoughtful. "Do men often flirt with women they have no intention of courting or marrying?"

Michael couldn't quite place the moment he had become Lady Patience's advisor on matters of the heart, but the role made him vastly uncomfortable. He raised one eyebrow as he recalled Lady Patience's behavior during her last visit. "Do women do the same with men?"

"No." Her voice was defensive.

Michael raised both eyebrows.

Her voice became flustered. "Well—er—yes, I suppose that is what *I* was doing. I have no intention of courting you, of course." Her cheeks turned a lovely shade of pink, a crack in her facade Michael hadn't yet seen. "I was practicing."

He threw her a teasing smile. "Ah, so women often practice their flirting on disposable men."

"You are not disposable." She scowled, straightening her chin. "Because you are painting my portrait."

Michael studied her flustered expression, hiding the smile that climbed his own face. He stepped behind the easel. "I am indeed, and I thank you for trusting me with the task. Before I begin today, would you like to see it? It is nearly complete."

Her eyes flew up to his, round and almost...terrified. Several seconds passed in silence before she spoke. "I—I suppose. I should ensure it is to my satisfaction before you continue." She stood abruptly, wringing her fingers together as she walked toward him.

Her nervousness must have been contagious. Michael's stomach had begun twisting. What if she didn't approve? His family needed her payment desperately, and he didn't know what he would do without it. He still had a fortnight before the marquess had scheduled his first appointment. There was some measure of security in that fact. He and his family and the studio could survive well enough on the remaining money from Mother's necklace until then.

Lady Patience stopped a few paces away. "P-perhaps I should wait until your work is entirely finished."

"Surely you must be curious," Michael said. In truth, he was curious to see her reaction. He turned his gaze back to the canvas, taking in the result of his hours and hours of work. The final details of Lady Patience's face had yet to be completed, but her hair and dress were finished. The portrait ended at her waist, and he had done all he could to showcase her perfect posture and long torso, and all the fine details of her gown. The lace on the ends of her long sleeves had been difficult, but he was proud of the result.

Now, to see if Lady Patience was proud of it as well.

He waved her forward, and she took one more step, those striking hazel eyes flooding with dread.

"You have nothing to fear, Lady Patience," he said with a laugh. "It would seem you assume I painted a monster."

Relief crashed over him when she smiled, just a hesitant curve at one corner of her mouth. "If that is what you see when you look at me, I should be greatly offended." Her smile only lasted a brief moment before she clamped her lips together, her throat bobbing with a swallow. Her pallor was concerning as she seemed to have one final debate with herself over whether or not to take the final few paces toward where Michael stood. Only from his angle was the portrait in full view. He stepped aside, making room for her to come stand where he stood.

With determination in her stride, she moved forward. The moment she did, Michael saw his discarded paintbrush on the floor. But he was too late. Lady Patience's foot made contact with the brush, and it rolled forward, throwing her off balance in the opposite direction. Michael had never seen anything but grace and perfection in her movements, but now she stumbled backward, her long limbs flailing.

He lunged forward to catch her, but not quickly enough. All he managed to reach was the fabric of her sleeve. A succinct series of popping threads cut through the air as the fabric tore, followed by a thud as Lady Patience hit the floor.

Michael rushed forward. Lady Patience sat up, her cheeks crimson. He squatted down beside her. "Are you hurt?" His gaze flickered over her in search of injuries. His eyes caught on her right arm, no longer covered by the thick sleeves she always wore. His gaze lingered on the large patches of puckered scars trailing from her wrist up to the middle of her upper arm. The skin was pale pink and white, scars grouped together like a spider's web, or the fragments of ice in a snowflake.

"No," Lady Patience whispered, angling her body away from him. Her mortification was obvious, and it wrenched at Michael's heart. She started to stand, and Michael reached for her hands to assist her. Her fingers shook. He pulled her to her feet, and the moment she was standing, she tugged her hands away from his. Her gaze flicked frantically around the room as she crossed her arms, attempting to hide the bare skin that her torn sleeve had exposed. Her cheeks were still pink as she lunged for the fabric on the floor, pulling it back up over her arm as best as she could. It hung from her elbow, loose threads dangling from the edge.

Michael searched her face. "Are you certain you aren't hurt? Forgive me, I should have ensured the path was clear before insisting you walk forward."

She refused to look at him, crossing her opposite arm over her body to hold the torn sleeve in place. She didn't say a word.

Emma and Isabel had seen the incident unfold, and they were now rushing toward them, offering Lady Patience anything from tea to water to biscuits. Michael wished he could reassure her somehow, but he didn't want to draw attention to the fact that he had seen the scars on her arm. Would it lessen her humiliation if he told her that he was not disgusted by them? He decided it would be better not to speak of them at all.

She remained silent, scowling down at the floor.

"My lady—"

"I am well," she snapped, eyes blazing. With a determined stride, she walked forward, still clutching her arms against herself. She turned to face the canvas, the horror in her gaze intensifying.

Michael held his breath while she stared at the portrait. The color in her cheeks remained as she whirled toward him. "This is not what I asked for."

He frowned, heart beating in his throat. "I don't understand."

"I asked for a three-quarter." Her voice was frantic, edged with anger.

"This is a three-quarter." Michael gestured at the portrait.

"No." She shook her head, ringlets thrashing. Her dark brows drew together. "The portrait only depicts me from the waist and above. That is certainly not three-quarters."

Michael rubbed one side of his face, catching Isabel's gaze from behind Lady Patience. His two sisters watched the ordeal with wide eyes and slack jaws. "You must have been misinformed," he said. "A three-quarter portrait means the canvas is three-quarters of a yard in size."

She breathed deeply, eyes glistening. "You should have explained the difference to me! How should I know about these matters? You are the artist, and I am the client. It is too small. My father will not hang this in the gallery." Her voice grew harder but quieter—a harsh whisper. "I will not pay for this."

Michael's stomach fell, a wave of anger gripping his chest. "You acted so certain that a three-quarter was what you wanted. You did not question me about what the dimensions would be. I cannot read your mind."

Her eyes sparked dangerously. "I have no use for a portrait this size."

"Please reconsider—"

"No. I told you I would not pay for it if I was not satisfied, and you agreed."

Michael groaned, unable to remain courteous. Panic had set into his bones, especially with his two sisters staring at him. They needed this money. "Lady Patience, your lack of satisfaction with it is entirely your own fault. You cannot cast all the blame on me. It seems that what you wanted was a half-length. It is a larger canvas that depicts the subject to just below their knees."

"That is three-quarters of the subject, is it not? It doesn't make sense!" Her voice cracked.

"I know!" Michael gave an exasperated sigh, trying to regain his composure. "It is simply the way it is. If you needed an explanation, you might have asked for one."

She raised her chin. "I have never been treated so poorly at a business establishment. Why should this encourage me to pay you?" Holding her sleeve up with one hand, she marched past him. She fetched her bonnet and started toward the door.

"My lady—please forgive me. Allow me to start on a new portrait for you, this time in the size you need." Michael followed behind her, but stopped in his tracks when she turned on him.

"I wish to never come to this studio again, and I will ensure no one of my acquaintance comes either—especially not the marquess."

His nostrils flared, and his anxiety doubled. "Lord Clitheroe?"

"He is *the gentleman* of whom I have been speaking. I am the reason he scheduled an appointment with you at all, and now I shall be the reason he never sets foot here."

"Lady Patience, please."

She shook her head, refusing to so much as look at him again before marching out the door and letting it slam behind her.

Silence fell in the studio, and Michael watched Lady Patience's back through the window. Where was she going? The torn fabric of her sleeve rustled in the wind as she tore away from his studio more quickly than she would have had it been on fire.

Michael's face was on fire. His hands curled at his sides.

Emma and Isabel stood in stunned silence until Emma finally spoke. "If-if the marquess doesn't come, how will we afford the studio?"

He shook his head as dread fell through his chest. "I don't know." He had been relying on the marquess's recommendation. It could have changed their lives.

He had been wrong. He would still think of Lady Patience Hansford every day of his life. He would think of her when his family became hungry. He would think of her as he searched tirelessly for clients in town. But no matter how he thought of her, one thing was certain: He would no longer think of her with any measure of fondness.

CHAPTER EIGHT

*H*ot tears rolled down Patience's face as she ran out into the street. Her vision flashed in white as she found her way behind an alley. Pressing her back against the neighboring establishment, she hid her face in her hands. Not only was she humiliated by the fact that Mr. Cavinder had seen her scars, but she was even more humiliated by the way she had reacted.

Her emotions had taken hold of her in a way they never had before. She had been cruel and unkind when she saw that the portrait was not what she had expected. His work had been extraordinary, yet she had berated him for all the flaws of the piece that had nothing to do with the actual likeness. Fear had struck her heart like an arrow at full speed. Not only was the portrait too small to hang in the gallery, but it was surely more beautiful than she was.

Her mind replayed the moment she had fallen and her sleeve had torn. She squeezed her eyes closed. Mr. Cavinder had stared at her arm for several seconds. He had *stared,* just as Mama had said people would. The instruction Mama had given her over the years since the incident that caused the burns had been to *keep them hidden. Keep them covered. No one will wish to be near you if they see them. No one will respect you. No one could love you. It is better that you wear long sleeves. Longer gloves.*

Wear your blue pelisse to the cricket match.

Patience had done all she could to obey. No one had seen her scars in the ten years since they had come to exist. Not until today.

And she would have preferred that anyone see them but Mr. Cavinder. Her heart stung and her cheeks burned. Her veins still ran hot with anger. Mr. Cavinder had been so defensive and impertinent. She narrowed her eyes as she looked up at the rain spiraling from the sky. As much as she wished she could blame him, she couldn't. She could only blame herself.

It was better that Mr. Cavinder think badly of her, even if she could hardly bear the thought. At least she wouldn't wonder if he had any sort of attachment to her, especially now that he had also seen her scars. She wouldn't fill her mind during idle hours of his handsome dark eyes and wide smile. It had been a silly infatuation. No, she wouldn't even call it that. She had enjoyed his company. The time she had spent in his studio had been freeing, safe, and comfortable, even despite the fact that she had to hold a pose for hours at a time. It was strange, but she would miss it.

Mr. Cavinder had been a distraction she did not need. All her attention needed to be on Lord Clitheroe, nothing else.

No one else.

———— ⌒ ————

Lord Clitheroe invited Patience's family to dinner the following week, and he was just as attentive as he had been before. His attentiveness did not end with Patience, however. He seemed to be just as captivated with Hattie—if not even more so. Patience tried to ignore the growing dread in her stomach, but it persisted throughout the meal.

When the men joined the women in the drawing room, Lord Clitheroe came to sit beside Patience. She searched for something to say to fill the silence. "I trust you have had an enjoyable week?" she asked.

"Not as enjoyable as it might have been, had I seen you at least once." He flashed a flirtatious smile.

Patience glanced at Mama, who was not being discreet about her eavesdropping. She returned her attention to Lord Clitheroe, struggling to find something flirtatious to say in return. "I—would agree, my lord." She cringed at the lack of wit she had when under pressure. If only she had several minutes to think of a reply; she was certain she could have come up with something genius.

"What has been the most enjoyable part of your week?" Lord Clitheroe asked.

Patience tried to lean closer, but the sight of the

marquess's half-closed eyes was far too unsettling. She remained stiff. "Well—I have been helping my sister prepare for her wedding. She will be married in a fortnight."

The marquess's gaze shifted to Hattie, a distant look in his gaze. He pressed his lips together, peeling his gaze away from Hattie with great effort, before it settled on Patience again. "What an excellent wedding it will be. You must be very happy for your sister."

"Indeed." Patience swallowed, interlocking her fingers on her lap.

"Is your portrait complete? I have been most eager to see it."

The question made Patience's stomach drop. She had been trying very hard not to think of Mr. Cavinder and the entire portrait ordeal. "No...I'm afraid I am no longer having my portrait painted."

"Why ever not?" The marquess's fluffy hair flopped to one side as he observed her with surprise.

"He painted the wrong size. I did not wish to invest more time in having it corrected." Shame climbed her cheeks as she thought again of her behavior the week before.

"Oh, dear." Lord Clitheroe clucked his tongue and crossed one ankle over his knee. "I will cancel my appointment with him promptly then. Such a mistake cannot be excusable."

Patience shook her head. "That is not necessary, my

lord. You might not experience the same difficulties as I did."

He scoffed. "I will not trust such a new painter if he is not highly recommended by an acquaintance of mine. Seeing as you did not receive the product you wished for, I don't see any reason that I should keep my appointment with him."

It would not be wise to argue with the marquess, so she simply nodded in agreement, throwing a coy smile into the gesture. "You are very wise, my lord."

He gave a smug smile, his eye twitching in a wink. "I am indeed. Although my wisdom can often betray me."

She frowned. "How so?"

"It was my wisdom which led me to accept an invitation from an old friend who is currently in India. I will be traveling there next week for business matters which I will not bore you with. It pains me to inform you that I will not return to England for nine months." He sighed. "The most central source of my regret, my lady, is that I will not be near you and your family for such a long period of time."

Patience's heart pounded in her throat. *Nine months?* Mama would be horribly disappointed to hear that. Patience hadn't even known Lord Clitheroe for nine months, so he would easily forget her by the time he returned to England. All that she had dared to hope for came crashing down around her. "Well, my lord…we expect you to call upon us the moment you return."

"You have my word." He grinned, leaning his elbows

on his knees. Patience followed his gaze, not surprised to find it lingering on Hattie once again.

Patience's chest tightened, but she reminded herself that it was she who he had chosen to sit beside. But how could she spend the next nine months waiting for Lord Clitheroe's return? There was no understanding between them. It now made sense that he hadn't tried to court her. If he was leaving so soon, it would have been inconsiderate to have done so. She hoped that explanation would appease Mama.

When the evening drew to a close and Patience and her family departed in their coach, Lord Clitheroe whispered to Patience in passing. "Farewell, my lady. Until we meet again."

"Farewell, my lord." She cast him a demure grin, one that had taken a great deal of practice.

The smile Hattie gave him as she passed was similar, but with a much more professional execution.

As expected, Mama was furious to hear of Lord Clitheroe's sudden departure. As soon as they were within the carriage and rolling away from the marquess's estate, Mama crossed her arms with a huff, turning to face Papa. "How dare Lord Clitheroe leave us?"

"The man can do as he wishes," Papa muttered, glancing at his reflection in the carriage window. He combed his fingers over his thick side whiskers. "He would not stay in England only for Patience." He chuckled. "No indeed."

Patience looked out the window, tightening her jaw.

When he returned, she would prove to them all that he did want to court her. She had nine months to prepare, and when Lord Clitheroe saw her again, he would be unable to resist her. He would come begging for her hand.

She banished her doubt and fear. It had never given her anything. No matter what, she would prove her family wrong. She would finally be what they had always wished for her to be. She closed her eyes, schooling her heart into submission. No matter what anyone said, she would not allow it to affect her. It didn't matter if her family didn't believe in her. They never had, after all. She needed only to believe in herself.

In nine months, Lord Clitheroe would return, and in ten months, she was determined to be engaged to him.

CHAPTER NINE

*T*he sound of tearing paper was not as satisfying as Michael had hoped, even after tearing the letter five times. He let the pieces fall to the floor before sitting down beside them, burying his face in his hands. He let out an exasperated sigh, dragging his fingers down his cheeks.

The letter had contained just what he feared. The marquess's cancelation of his appointment.

Lady Patience was nothing if not thorough. She could not ruin his business half-heartedly, no, that would have been too kind.

His family had been distraught enough to hear of Lady Patience's cancelation. What would they think when they learned that she had advised the marquess to cancel too? Perhaps what hurt the most was that his mother had sold her necklace for nothing. His father's health was growing worse by the day. The physician had told their family that he was only expected to live a few more weeks. Michael's chest had been aching ever since he had heard that news. His anxiety had been potent.

He glared at the place where he had left Lady Patience's portrait on his easel. Her beauty was deceiving, and he couldn't deny that he had fallen victim to it. He had failed to see what she was capable of. She was selfish and cruel, just like her father. Portraits depicted only the best of people, but Lady Patience had shown him her worst. If only it were something that could be depicted in art. Instead, he was instructed to portray only ideals, beauty, and perfection. If he could portray Lady Patience's heart, what would be on that canvas?

His own words to Lady Patience from the last time he had seen her echoed through his mind.

"*It would seem you assume I painted a monster,*" Michael had said when she had been afraid to approach the canvas.

The world outside his shop was dark, his studio windows lit only by a half-moon and a sprinkling of stars. He hadn't been sleeping well of late, so he had been coming to his studio to practice.

Tonight, something drew him to his unfinished portrait of Lady Patience. He would have no use for it now that she would not purchase it. He couldn't bear to dispose of it after all his hard work, but he also couldn't bear to look at her appearing so perfect and beautiful. How many people in the world existed the way Lady Patience did? Surely everyone, if their souls were laid bare, would be depicted a little differently than they appeared on the outside.

He walked toward Lady Patience's portrait, examining it from all angles as an idea twisted through his mind. This idea would be far more satisfying than tearing paper.

Working quickly, he began mixing his paints, organizing his brushes, and adding several adjustments to Lady Patience's portrait. On one half of her face, he darkened her eye, taking away the brightness and color that had been there before. He deepened the arch of her eyebrow, bringing a wicked gleam to the expression on one half of her face. He added gray to the tone of her skin on that same half, eliminating the warm, flushed glow he had given her before.

He released the reins on his creativity—and, admittedly —his bitterness. He worked through the entire night, hardly pausing as he added the horrific details to the piece. A horn on one side of her head. A leathery ear. Protruding teeth in the shape of fangs. The other half of her face remained tranquil and breathtakingly beautiful. The contrast was shocking, and when the first hints of dawn spilled through his windows, Michael stood back to admire his work.

The message was clear. Beauty is dangerous, and it is not to be trusted. Where beauty could be a reflection of one's equally beautiful soul, it could also be a disguise for a monstrous one.

Michael had never painted something so uncommon

and unsightly. People did not look upon art to be disgusted, but somehow he didn't think people would be disgusted by this portrait. They would be intrigued. It was a thought-provoking piece, and even though he had just spent hours painting it, Michael couldn't stop staring at the canvas as morning light spilled through the windows, reflecting off of the wet paint on the right side of Lady Patience's likeness. The monstrous side.

Surprisingly, the activity had managed to lessen his frustration and anxiety. He took a deep breath, still in awe that so many hours had passed. He had never been so immersed in a project before. His emotions had never been so involved. Exhaustion had begun to set in, so he put away his brushes and turned the canvas away and out of sight before starting toward home.

His back ached and his eyes stung, but he managed to smile as he walked through the door of their apartment. Mother was cooking breakfast while the others in the house likely still slept.

"Where on earth have you been?" she asked, a thread of shock in her voice. "I thought you were asleep in your bed all this time."

"I've been painting." He walked with casual steps to inspect the eggs she was cooking. His stomach growled.

Mother cast him a sideways glance. "Is it work for another client?" The hope in her voice broke his heart.

"I'm afraid not." He sighed. "It was a creative piece of my own. I—well, I very much enjoyed completing it."

"You still need to sleep." Mother's brow furrowed.

"It is always beneficial to practice my craft." He picked up a piece of egg from the corner of her pan, blowing on it gently before popping it in his mouth.

Mother didn't object, but instead, she offered him the entire pan. He shook his head, laughing. "Father will have my head if he knows I ate all his eggs."

A slight smile pulled on her lips. "I suppose you are right. He is already awake." Her features drooped. "He has been in a great deal of pain and has had difficulty sleeping." She scooped the eggs onto a plate, adding a slice of bread and cup of water. "Will you take his breakfast to him?"

Michael nodded, his own expression turning solemn. Pain radiated out from his heart, tingling in his limbs as he ascended the narrow, creaking staircase to Father's room. Father appeared to be sleeping at first glance, but the moment the door opened, so did his eyes. He surveyed Michael with furrowed brows. The corners of his mouth twitched as he groaned. "I have told your mother never to trust you with my breakfast tray. You will have eaten three-quarters of it on the way up the stairs."

Michael wanted to laugh, but the sound lodged in his throat. he was not particularly fond of the words *three-quarters* at the moment. And he would miss his father's slightly insulting comments.

"You are fortunate I didn't eat the entire plate. I'm hungry enough to eat three. I've been up all night paint-ing." He had to tell someone about his project. His father, being as artistic and creative as Michael was, would understand.

"Have you?" Father's eyes sparked with interest as he wriggled in the blankets, struggling to sit up. His frail frame was engulfed in the pillows behind him. "What is this piece that demands so much of your time?"

"It is not for a client," Michael said. It would be better to crush Father's hopes immediately. "It is a revision I have made to Lady Patience's portrait. It is unconventional and strange, but I am quite proud of the result. Of course, I would never show it to a soul."

"Not even this old soul?" Father pointed a slender finger at his own chest.

Michael laughed. "I suppose I could. It is drying in the studio at present."

"Fetch it for me as soon as you can. You know I cannot go without my curiosity being appeased on any matter." He sipped from his water cup, and Michael reached forward to steady his shaking hand.

"I will." Now that his father was so close to death, Michael would do anything he asked of him, if only to make up for all the times in his life that he hadn't. Panic began to set in as Michael remembered that he would soon be on his own. He would no longer have his father to advise him. Mother, Emma, and Isabel relied on him, and he had already failed once. How many more times would he fail? "Father, I'm afraid," Michael said in a quiet voice. "I don't know if I will be able to find any more clients. I-I don't know if I will be able to provide for our family."

"You will." Father did not hesitate. "I have no doubt that your talents will be discovered. You are a good man, Michael. You must expect good things to come into your life."

"Life is not always so just or generous as that." How could Father believe such a thing when he himself was a good man, yet his own life was drawing to a close years before it should have?

"Life is not always generous, but hard work and determination will give you far more than you realize."

Michael let the words settle into his bones. He would never stop working to make his family feel secure and comfortable. Though he was skeptical, he chose to believe his father's wisdom. It calmed the turmoil in his chest. "Is it the eggs that are giving you such wisdom?" Michael asked. "Perhaps I should have eaten them on my way up the stairs after all."

"If you had, I wouldn't be speaking to you at all." Father took a small bite, throwing Michael a smirk.

They talked for nearly an hour, and at the end of their visit, Father raised a hand above his blankets. "Please do not forget to bring me the painting. I do wish to see it."

Michael nodded. "I won't forget."

How could he forget that piece? The image was still vivid in his mind—Lady Patience Hansford, half beauty, half monster. She was leaning off of a precipice, teetering between both identities. Michael thought of the scars on her arm, the horror in her eyes when he had seen them. There was more to Lady Patience than what met the eye, and though Michael had been hurt by her, he suspected she was not entirely wicked. She was much like that painting. Soon, one side or the other would triumph, either the beauty engulfing the monster, or the monster devouring the beauty. He could only hope, for her sake, that it was the former.

———————— ᝰ ————————

When Michael's revised portrait was finally dry a week later, he wrapped it up and took it to Father's bedchamber. His heart pounded as he uncovered the canvas. He peeked out from behind it, holding his breath as he awaited Father's reaction. Slowly, a smile crept over Father's face, his eyes rounding as he beckoned Michael closer.

"How fascinating." He squinted, tipping his head to one side. "The lady's mask has come undone."

"Precisely." Michael took a deep breath. "I have tried to convey that message."

"You have succeeded." Father coughed into his blanket, his eyes filling with tears from the strain. He blinked them away, focusing on the portrait again.

"This is masterful, Michael, and I do not say that lightly."

Pride flooded Michael's heart, and an odd surge of emotion made his throat clench. "You taught me all I know."

"What you did with this portrait cannot be taught,"

Father said in a raspy voice. He cleared his throat. "It is extraordinary talent."

Michael studied the portrait again. He had heard that any form of art was strengthened by emotion. So many times he had painted without emotion, simply applying methodical strokes to a canvas. This had been different. His fear and worry and anger had all poured out of his heart, reflecting back as this work of art. He could hardly take credit for it.

"Michael." Father's voice took on a new tone, one even more serious than before. "I will die soon."

The plainness of his words drove a dagger into Michael's heart.

Father coughed again, rolling to the side to face Michael more fully. "That misfortune comes with a few privileges." A weak smile pulled on the wrinkles around his mouth.

"Privileges?" Michael raised his eyebrows.

"The right of a dying person is to present their last wishes to their family members and expect them to be fulfilled." Father touched the corner of the canvas that Michael still held in front of him. "I have a wish that I would like you to fulfill for me."

"Anything, Father." Michael nodded for him to continue.

"I would like you to submit this piece to the exhibition at the Royal Academy. The exhibition is next spring. You will receive word a month or two before the exhibition if your piece is to be included or not."

Michael laughed under his breath. "This piece is not worthy of a London exhibition. It is far too...unconventional."

"People in London are always in search of something to flap their tongues about. They want to be surprised." Father gripped Michael's wrist. "This is the piece they have been searching for."

Michael shook his head, still far too hesitant to agree. "I cannot exploit Lady Patience's face in such a public manner."

"Call it revenge, if you will." Father's eyes gleamed with mischief.

"Father—" Michael shook his head as another laugh escaped him. The sound lodged in his throat as Father squeezed his wrist tighter.

"It is my final wish for you. Please, submit the piece. I daresay it could change the course of your life."

Michael turned his head to look at the portrait again. The odds of it being accepted were slim, and the odds of Lady Patience being recognized by the guests at the exhibition were even slimmer. Father was right—if it were accepted, his troubles could be lessened greatly. The exposure that such a display would bring him was incomparable.

"Very well. I will do it for you." Michael gave his promise, heart pounding against his ribs.

Father's frame seemed to relax, and he nestled his head into the pillows. He stared at the canvas for several seconds. "May I name the piece for you? It must be something all those who are in London will understand and find amusing."

"By all means." Michael studied the beautiful half of Lady Patience's likeness, then the other side. He couldn't decide which was more captivating.

Father grinned. "Let us call it *The Monstrous Debutante*."

CHAPTER TEN

TEN MONTHS LATER
Spring, 1817

Lord Clitheroe was a little more handsome than Patience remembered him being. Perhaps his time aboard the ship in the sunshine had aided the color of his complexion. However, all the time spent squinting at the sun might have been what made his eyes droop even more than they had before. But none of that mattered. No, indeed—all that mattered was that Lord Clitheroe had been courting her for the last month.

He had been courting *her*.

At least, that was how it appeared. He had left flowers for her soon after his return to England. Then, when Papa had invited him to dinner, he had asked Patience to join him for a ride the following day. Since then, they had gone on a picnic, a stroll around the royal crescent, and many more rides through town. Patience's work had paid off, it seemed.

She had spent nine months improving her flirting abilities. She had allowed Mama to coach her as she had always tried to. Patience had learned to *be patient* in waiting for the marquess to return and see who she had become. A smug smile climbed her lips. And now that Hattie was married, she did not have to worry about being overshadowed. Papa had even commissioned a new artist in town to paint a portrait of Patience, one that now hung in the gallery alongside all the other members of her family. For the first time in her life, she felt like she belonged.

The marquess had requested a private audience with her that day. She wore the pendant Mama had purchased for her in town nearly a year before. She considered it fondly as a lucky charm. She held it close to her chest, rubbing the cool metal against her neck. Her palms had been perspiring ever since she had heard the news that the marquess was coming. She wiped at her hairline and beneath her lower lip, clearing away the perspiration that had gathered there as well. Why was she so blasted hot? They were still on the coattails of winter, with spring just a few weeks away. She sat down on the settee in the drawing room at Briarwood just seconds before the door swung open and Lord Clitheroe was announced.

He stepped through the doors, bowing with a flourish. "There you are, my dear."

He had started calling her my dear during their last

ride. Patience found it rather charming. In all her days, she had rarely felt dear to anyone. To know that Lord Clitheroe held her in such high regard was comforting in a way she could not explain. "Good day, my lord." Patience smiled, taking his hands when he reached her. "What has brought you here?"

He traced a finger over her cheek, and she resisted the urge to lean back. *Stop*, she demanded herself. Why on earth would she wish to pull away? This was a marquess, after all, and he was in love with her. He had not put it into words yet, but his actions indicated as much. Her heart thudded at the possibility that he might propose to her. How proud would Mama be? How envious would Hattie be, knowing she had married lower than Patience had?

"My dear Patience, I think you already know." He winked, his gaze sweeping over her. "I have come to express my utmost admiration for you and request your hand in marriage."

Patience blinked, studying his smug grin. It truly was ever-present. Was that all he wished to say? She might have missed his proposal if she hadn't been listening closely enough. "Yes." Patience nearly jumped on her toes. "Yes, I will marry you."

Lord Clitheroe's grin widened. Patience could hardly comprehend what had just happened. Her heart thudded. Where was Mama? She had to tell her at once. When Patience looked up at the marquess's face again, she caught him staring at her lips. Would he kiss her now? This was the first time they had been alone together without a chaperone, and they had just become engaged, hadn't they? If there were ever a perfect moment to receive her first kiss, it was this moment.

The marquess licked his lips, leaning closer. Patience felt that same instinct to lean back as she had before, but she stiffened her muscles, forcing herself not to pull away from him. There were many women who found Lord Clitheroe attractive. So why should she not find him attractive as well?

He threaded his fingers behind her hair and pressed his lips against hers. She stood perfectly still, doing all she could to kiss him in return. She listened to her heart, seeking the sensation she had expected to feel while being kissed. Exhilaration, passion, joy, longing, *anything*. But her chest felt hollow, like an abandoned bird's nest in winter. Empty. Cold like Lord Clitheroe's lips.

She was thinking far too much of the specifics. She had nothing to compare this kiss to, so perhaps this was simply what a kiss felt like. She banished every stitch of disappointment that threaded through her stomach.

Lord Clitheroe pulled away, a gleam in his eyes that unsettled her stomach further. She shook the feeling away, replacing it with a sense of hope. No one had ever wanted her before. It was a new experience, one that she hesitated to hold onto. What if he changed his mind?

They walked out of the drawing room to find her parents, intent to tell them the happy news. They did not have to wander far to find them. Mama had been listening in the hall nearby, and Papa was immediately pulled out of his office by his wife.

"This day could not become any better," Mama said, resting a hand on her chest. "I have also just received word that Hattie will be coming to visit for an entire fortnight while her husband is away. Perhaps she can assist us with wedding preparations. She will be arriving in three weeks' time."

Patience swallowed. Why must Hattie always come to visit in the springtime? Patience hadn't yet checked on the nest in the tree yet, but she suspected it was too early for the bird to lay her eggs. She was likely safe, but she would have to check every morning during the fortnight of Hattie's visit so long as she brought her cat Aphrodite. She would not risk the birds being harmed again.

Papa offered his congratulations before striding back to the fencing room. He had been practicing his agility for the next cricket match that he planned to hold during the upcoming spring. This year, he was determined not to be struck in the face, or anywhere else for that matter.

"When shall we marry? In a fortnight?" she asked. That would give her time to wed before Hattie even arrived. She would prefer to be away on her wedding trip before Hattie could come to Briarwood.

The marquess chuckled. "Patience, my dear, you do not live up to your name."

His words echoed in her mind, bringing an old conversation back to the surface. Nearly a year ago, Mr. Cavinder had said something similar. She hadn't meant to, but she had thought of him often over the months since. She had seen his studio in the streets in town, abandoned and quiet. Each time she walked by, guilt whipped at her back. Where had he gone? Was she the reason his shop was closed?

She feared she would never know the answer.

She also feared to *know* the answer. Reflecting on her time spent in his studio brought a certain fondness to her heart. She did not have many memories that she held with fondness. It was strange that she would recall those days happily when she had ended them so harshly. It hurt to imagine what Mr. Cavinder thought of her.

The sound of Mama's laughter shocked Patience out of her reverie. Mama's laugher was rare, and it only presented itself when in the company of rich gentlemen. "Well, I suppose it is quite ironic that I gave such a name to my impatient child. Hattie is far more inclined to the virtue. I should have named her Patience instead."

Lord Clitheroe gave a slow grin, his own eyes glazing over in thought. "We shall marry in one month. Do you approve of that? In that case, your sister may be in town for the wedding."

Patience nodded, even though a knot formed in her stomach. Why was she feeling so ill? She had nothing to dread. This was what she had always dreamed of. "If I must learn to be patient, then I suppose I must practice." She took a deep breath. "I will wait one more month."

What Lord Clitheroe failed to remember was that she had already waited nine while he was away, and now ten. She had been anticipating his return, and she had successfully caught him. She was far more patient than she used to be, and it had worked in her favor. In one month, she would finally have achieved her greatest dream.

So why did she still feel so hollow inside?

———————— ✿ ————————

"Michael!" Emma and Isabel came running across the stone path in front of their apartment, holding up their skirts to avoid tripping on the uneven stones. Isabel held a letter in her hand, waving it above her head like a flag.

"What is it?" He was grateful for the distraction from the pain in his back. He had been assisting his friend, a cordwainer, in his shop all day for a small payment. It was how he had spent the last nine months—scraping up meager bits of work where he could. Aside from offering assistance to established shopkeepers in town who had known his father and took pity on Michael, he had also managed to gather a few pupils to whom he taught art lessons each week. But even despite all his efforts, he had lost the studio, and they had nearly lost their apartment.

Even now, as Emma and Isabel ran toward him, their hems were torn and dirty.

"It is a letter from the Royal Academy," Emma said, out of breath. She and Isabel exchanged an eager glance, the symmetry of the movement rather unsettling.

Michael chuckled, though his heart was in his throat. It had been so long since he had submitted his portrait of Lady Patience—*The Monstrous Debutante,* as Father had named it. The only reason he had submitted it at all was to fulfill Father's dying wish. After he had died, eight months before, Michael had finally sent the painting to the Royal Academy. He had never expected it to be accepted, so he had no hope in the letter that Isabel eagerly extended to him.

"It is likely a courtesy letter to inform me that the painting was not accepted." Michael hadn't allowed himself to hope for anything for months, not since he lost the two clients whose recommendations could have set off a lifetime of success as a painter. He had fallen too far to ever dare climb so high again.

"Open it, open it!" Isabel thrust the letter into his hand. "If Papa were here his curiosity would exceed all of ours. I daresay he is even watching over us right now, and soon enough he will come in spirit and open the letter himself."

Michael laughed at the accuracy of her words. Father would have torn the letter open long before Michael even had a chance to see it.

"Very well, I'll open it." He tore the seal, unfolding the paper. His fingers shook and his heart raced, which meant he had not been entirely honest with himself.

He might have still had a little hope.

His eyes skimmed over the words, jumping to the most important phrase.

We are pleased to inform you that your piece, The Monstrous Debutante, has been selected to be displayed at the Exhibition of the Royal Academy.

"It has been accepted," Michael muttered, reading the entire page again. "It has been accepted!" He looked up, raking a hand over his hair. He paused to breathe, shaking his head. "It says here that it will be displayed on the lower level where it may be viewed at a closer proximity by all who attend."

Emma and Isabel began jumping, clapping their hands together with glee. "May we come with you to London?" Isabel asked. "I have always wanted to go to London."

"As have I," Emma added, eyes gleaming.

Michael rubbed his jaw, hardly listening to the requests that poured from his sisters' mouths. His pulse still pounded past his ears. The sort of people who would be attending the exhibition would be wealthy and influential. If his painting could capture their attention, then he could have a list of clients too long to manage. He might finally feel that his family's future was secure. A small part of him —a very small part—still worried over using Lady Patience's likeness in such a public way. He quickly banished the concern.

It was Lady Patience's wickedness that had first ruined them, so now, perhaps, it would be her wickedness portrayed in that painting that would save them.

It was only fair, after all. What harm could it possibly do?

CHAPTER ELEVEN

*P*atience stuck her finger with the needle she had been embroidering with. She pulled it back, pinching the dot of blood between her two fingers. She nearly thrust her embroidery hoop across the room in frustration. She hadn't been able to focus, not since Hattie had arrived at Briarwood.

She had been there for two days, and she had already changed at least half of Patience's wedding plans according to her own preference. Patience had allowed it since Mama had shared Hattie's opinion.

She reined in her frustration. All that mattered was that Patience was marrying Lord Clitheroe; it didn't matter how or where or when. Since her engagement, Mama had begun speaking to her differently. Her voice lacked the pity and condescension it had always carried before. Every time she spoke of Patience's engagement, however, her voice carried a tone of surprise.

"I never thought Patience would secure such an advantageous match," she had said earlier that very day, before Patience had entered the drawing room. Patience had stopped outside the door when she had heard her name, listening to the conversation within. Between the crack of the partially closed door, Patience had seen Hattie nod her agreement—a slow nod—the sort that is used when one cannot comprehend the possibility of something. "I must confess I was shocked to hear the news. If only I had found an opportunity to meet Lord Clitheroe before I accepted Lord Bampton's proposal."

Patience had hardly believed what she had heard. Was Hattie not pleased enough with her own marriage to an earl? Patience's face had grown hot, but she had allowed it to cool before entering the room.

The rest of the afternoon had passed slowly, and Patience had spent most of it alone in the drawing room. She had been trying not to dwell on the events of the previous evening—the first of Hattie's visit—but the memory had been weighing down on her chest like a boulder.

Hattie had whispered something to Lord Clitheroe. He had smiled. Then he had looked around the room. Hattie's hand had lingered on his arm before she had walked away.

Patience had excused the exchange as nothing more than a friendly remark in passing, but her heart had been behaving wildly of late, inventing scenarios meant to scare her. Hattie and Lord Clitheroe would be part of the same family soon. Sister and brother-in-law. There was nothing more to what she had seen. She had to believe that.

———————⁓———————

Early the next morning, Patience draped her cloak over her shoulders, pulling it around herself and over the scars on her arm. A shudder ran over her skin as the cold air of the morning seeped through her windowsill. Her arm had been more sensitive to things both hot and cold ever since she had been injured ten years before. With her wedding approaching, Mama had instructed her to be even more diligent in keeping her arms hidden. An annulment, Mama had said, would be a far greater task than breaking off an engagement. When Lord Clitheroe saw her arm, it would have to be after they were married. At that point, he would not be able to run away.

Patience wrung her fingers together to warm them. She closed her eyes, pressing down the anxiety that rose in her chest. Even if he did not run, it was terrifying to think that he would wish to. She didn't want anyone to feel trapped with her. She wanted to be *loved*.

Her heart stung.

That was all she had ever wanted. Did Mama love her now? Did Papa? Hattie?

Her gaze caught on the tree at the edge of the lawn. Pacing nearby was a creature covered in fur and a long tail. Aphrodite. She was prowling for eggs, no doubt.

Patience had forgotten to check the tree all week to

ensure that the bird had not laid her eggs yet. It was still early in the spring, but Patience could not take any risks. She hurried out the door and across the lawn. With her arms outstretched, she sneaked up behind the cat, scooping it off the ground. It clawed at her exposed wrists, hissing at her.

"Oh, hush." Patience said. "You—"

She paused when she heard a rustle behind the tree. A quiet whisper. Deep laughter.

Her head felt light, her legs heavy as she walked closer. Her heart was like a hammer against her ribs, striking pain with each beat.

She peeked between the leaves. Hattie's back was pressed against a tree, her arms wrapped around Lord Clitheroe's neck. He leaned down to kiss her, and she did not object, pulling him closer by the lapels.

Patience's heart jumped to her throat. She couldn't watch another second of the scene unfold. Emotion seared across her body, and she nearly crumbled where she stood. Patience had known Hattie was wicked in some respects, but she had never expected her to be capable of *this*.

There she stood, blissfully betraying Patience and her own husband, and likely not for the first time.

Patience hadn't realized she was squeezing Aphrodite. The cat hissed again, sinking its teeth into the side of her hand. She dropped the creature, and it darted into the trees, straight toward the place where Hattie still kissed her sister's betrothed. Shamelessly. Heartlessly.

Patience backed away, nearly tripping over the back of

her cloak. What Aphrodite had done to the birds was nothing compared to this. Hattie was the true monster.

The blade of betrayal was sharpest of them all, and it cut her straight through her center. She could hardly breathe amid the sobs that shook her as she ran back to the house. No one saw her. She managed to slip into her room without being caught. She sat on the floor of her bedchamber—there seemed no more suitable place than that. Pulling her knees into her chest, she buried her face in them.

She had always considered herself skilled at keeping secrets, but this would be the most painful to keep. If she told anyone what she had seen, chaos would ensue. Hattie's husband could challenge the marquess to a duel—even one to the death. But if she kept this secret, Lord Clitheroe might still marry her. She would still be the wife of a marquess, even if he did not love her in return. Her future would still be secure. If she didn't marry him, would she ever receive another offer? The thought of spending her days in spinsterhood with her parents nearly broke her in two. They would resent her. They would disapprove of her far more than she could bear.

Pain spiraled through her chest. She would do all she could to forget what she had seen. It was not worth losing all that she had worked for for nearly an entire year. She hardened the walls around her heart, wiping angrily at her tears.

She would still marry the marquess, even if she had to bury her heart in order to do it.

Lady Patience looked even more frightening by candlelight. The right side of her face at least.

Michael stood back as the crowds at the exhibition encircled the portrait, whispering to one another and gasping in what Michael hoped was delight—and a bit of surprise.

The exhibition was more grand that Michael remembered it. He had attended the exhibition once, many years before, with his father. He had come as a spectator, not as a participating artist. He could recall the day he attended and the dreams that had been circling through his heart ever since. He had promised himself that one day he would see a piece of his work displayed in those grand halls. He had never expected it would come about the way it had.

He looked up, letting his senses soak in the grandeur of his surroundings. Ornate frames lined the walls from floor to ceiling, works of all sizes laid within them. A large chandelier hung at the center of the room, casting the glow of hundreds of candles over the dried paint, making it shine and return to life. He surveyed the rest of the room. Of the many guests in attendance that evening, the vast majority had begun gathering around *The Monstrous Debutante*, eager to see what had drawn so many eyes.

A voice stood out from the rest, coming from a tall man with greying hair. "This looks like the daughter of Lord Ryecombe," he said to the woman beside him. "I dined with their family once at Briarwood, and I am certain it is her."

Michael's stomach flopped. He had hoped she wouldn't be recognized. Many others walked closer to the piece, pointing out the fangs and eyes and all the other monstrosities they could find. It was what people of London society did best, after all, pointing out the flaws of others. If their masks were pulled back, what would be underneath?

His deep thoughts were interrupted by a man beside him, cane in hand. "Mr. Cavinder, is it?"

"I am." Michael bowed in greeting.

"Mr. Jones, a pleasure. Your work is extraordinary. Are you accepting clients? My family is due for new portraits. I would require half-lengths for myself, my wife, and my three sons."

Michael's throat went dry. *Speak, you fool.* He swallowed. "Yes, of course. I would be happy to provide your entire family with portraits."

"Capital! So long as you do not paint us as a family of monsters."

"I won't, so long as you all hold still and behave."

The man chuckled, pointing at the portrait on display. "Did this poor girl dare move a finger? Is that why she has earned the name of 'The Monstrous Debutante?'"

Michael looked down at his boots. "She did far more than that."

"Ah—did she break your heart?"

"No," Michael said under his breath. Though she had wounded it. He had dared to look for the best in her, but she had fooled him. He could not deny that he had been drawn to her, and it had hurt him to discover that she was as cruel and prideful as her father. "The story behind this piece is meant to remain a mystery," Michael finished.

"I see." The man rubbed his jaw before gazing at the portrait once again. "I look forward to seeing your talent at work with my family. How may I schedule our appointments?"

Michael hesitated, searching for a solution. He had traveled to London alone, renting a small apartment for the duration of the exhibition. His plan had been to attend the opening day in order to see how his work was received. He wasn't prepared to take clients in London yet, but here was a man requesting five portraits from him. He could not turn him down.

"Call upon me in a fortnight at this address." Michael handed the man a card from his pocket with the address of his rented apartment in London. "I am still in the process of—er—preparing my studio in town."

The man nodded, waving the card in front of him. "I will."

Michael smiled. "I thank you for your patience." The moment the word *patience* escaped his mouth, a shiver ran over his arms. Meeting Lady Patience Hansford could have very well been the best thing that had happened to him in his life. If this man's request was only the beginning, then he would need to make haste with his studio preparations. One fortnight was hardly enough time, but with enough determination, he could succeed.

His first step was to return to Inglesbatch to fetch his mother and two sisters. He had a feeling they would be in London for a long time.

The crowd of spectators surrounding the portrait grew as the night went on, and by the end of the evening, Michael had begun writing down names and addresses of his potential new clients as they came to speak with him.

One week later, his schedule was filled for the next five months.

And by the time a fortnight had passed, news of Lady Patience's portrait was printed in The Morning Chronicle, named the most admired piece of the exhibition. Gossip papers of all kinds had begun inventing stories behind the portrait, theories that Michael hoped wouldn't be believed. He was still grateful for them, ridiculous as they were, because they were what drew more people to the exhibition to see *The Monstrous Debutante* with their own eyes.

The final gossip paper to release, however, made Michael's skin go cold. The scandal mongers had found what they had been searching for.

The Identity of The Monstrous Debutante Discovered

Our dear friends, many sources have now indicated with great confidence that the woman depicted in the astonishing piece by Michael Cavinder is Lady Patience Hansford of Inglesbatch, the second daughter of the Earl of Ryecombe. Shall we assume she is as monstrous as she appears in her portrait? Stay far away from this deceiving beauty, dear ones. She may bite if you come too close.

CHAPTER TWELVE

With her wedding three days away, Patience had hardly been able to sleep. Every time her mind became idle, she thought of Hattie and Lord Clitheroe. She thought of the secretive way in which they looked at one another each time he joined them for dinner. She thought of the moment he had pulled Patience aside in the courtyard and kissed her as if he hadn't just kissed Hattie earlier the same day.

He did not seem inclined to cancel the wedding. He might have still cared for Patience, but Hattie was too great a temptation. If he could have them both, then that was what he would try to do.

No matter his reasoning, Patience still felt a rope wrapping around her body, binding her arms and legs and flattening her lungs until she could hardly breathe. Pain radiated from her heart with each pulse. There was never a time at any point in each day that she was not anxious.

She could endure this. There were only three more days until she would secure Mama and Papa's esteem forever, wealth, prestige, and happiness. That last word hung heavy in her mind, large and misshapen, like it didn't belong. It wasn't wise to dream of happiness. There would always be something to make her unhappy. While she could rejoice in her comfortable home and position in society, she would be constantly concerned with her husband's behavior. If she married him already knowing he was a cad, then perhaps she could avoid disappointment in the future.

She sat in front of the looking glass in her bedchamber, noting the bags around her eyes and the dark circles that had begun to form. She had never noticed such things on her face before. She rubbed at them before giving up and turning away from her reflection.

Just as she turned around, the door of her bedchamber burst open. Patience jumped, letting out an accidental gasp as Mama charged into the room. Her hair was askew, eyes wild with terror.

"Mama!" Patience jumped to her feet. "What on earth is the matter?" She had never seen her mother so uncollected before.

"*This,*" she spat, "This is the matter." She flung a newspaper toward Patience, chest heaving. "The entire town has been speaking of you and the gossip in the papers. Read it for yourself and then explain to me what the meaning of it all is." Mama's face was splotched in red. "The ridicule our family may now face because of you..." her voice trailed off.

Patience tugged the paper from Mama's hand, heart racing. She hadn't done anything wrong, had she? If there were ever a scandal to find its way into the gossip papers, it would have been about Hattie and Lord Clitheroe. Patience hadn't told a soul—unless the servants had seen something and spilled the gossip. Would Patience be blamed for it somehow?

Her throat felt dry as she looked over the stack of various papers. Confusion clouded her vision as she tried to make sense of it all. The Monstrous Debutante's identity? Had someone known her during her first season and given her that name?

"I do not understand," Patience read a few more sentences before Mama snatched the papers from her.

"I have read them all. There is an exhibition happening presently at the Royal Academy in London. A painting there, completed by a Mr. Michael Cavinder is supposed to have depicted you as a monstrous creature. It has been the most popular painting of the exhibition. All of London now knows you as *The Monstrous Debutante*, the daughter of the Earl of Ryecombe." Mama let out an anguished sigh. "Who is Mr. Cavinder? How did he create this portrait of you?"

Patience felt the color drain from her face. Her hands shook at her sides. Had Mr. Cavinder altered the portrait she had refused to pay him for? Was this his method of seeking revenge? She had felt guilty over what she had done to him, but all that guilt was now draining out of her heart like the color in her cheeks.

"Do you know him?" Mama's voice was laced with suspicion.

"He lives here in Inglesbatch." Patience's hands shook as she rubbed them over her skirts. "Before Papa commissioned my new portrait in the gallery, I went to Mr. Cavinder's studio. It was a long time ago. Nearly a year ago now." Patience caught her breath. "I-I was not satisfied with the result of the portrait, and so I did not pay him for it. I suppose this made him quite angry."

"Has he done this out of spite? The entirety of London now believes you to be a monster!" Mama's voice took on a shrieking tone. "If that is what he hoped to accomplish, then he has succeeded."

Patience's heart sank. Mr. Cavinder did indeed think as badly of her as she had imagined. But this was worse, far worse. She hadn't thought him to be the sort of man to seek revenge. It seemed she had misjudged him. How could he have been so cruel? Her reputation now hung by a thread. Mama acted as though their entire family might be affected.

"What am I to do?" Patience asked, her voice faint.

Mama glared at her. "There is nothing that can be done now. Because of your careless behavior toward Mr. Cavinder, you have brought ruin upon us all." Mama gripped Patience's shoulders. "Do you realize this?"

Patience cringed at the force of Mama's voice.

A light knock sounded on the half-opened door, and a maid peeked her head inside. Her eyes were round like the knots in the walnut wood of the door. "Lady Patience, the

Marquess of Clitheroe is awaiting you in the drawing room."

Patience nearly choked. What was he doing here? Mama jumped back, clutching both hands to her chest. "He must have seen the papers."

The lightness in Patience's head intensified, and she blinked hard to clear the moisture from her eyes. *Remain calm.* She stiffened her posture, tugging her sleeves up higher on her arms before rushing past Mama toward the door. "He likely has come for an explanation, that is all." She cast Mama a reassuring smile. Her mind raced with every doubt imaginable. Dread pooled in her stomach, making her ill. Why were her stays laced so tightly? Her lungs could barely expand as she made her way down the stairs.

Though she didn't say a word, Patience could hear Mama following her down to the drawing room. She waited in the hallway near the door as Patience slipped inside. Lord Clitheroe faced the window on the opposite side of the room, his back facing her. Patience closed the door behind her, adjusting her expression before turning around. It would be best to act as if nothing was amiss.

With a smile, she offered a curtsy. "What brings you here today, my lord?" She walked toward him. He had turned away from the window, a pained smile on his face. Her gaze froze on that expression, and her heart pinched. Ever since she had seen him kiss Hattie, a sense of heavy dread engulfed her each time she was near him. Every word, glance, and step was filled with caution.

"Surely you must know." He rubbed his hands on the sides of his leather breeches with a sigh. "I read the papers this morning."

She was silent for several seconds. "It is gossip. You do not believe it, do you?"

"The Morning Chronicle published the news as well. It is a reputable source. At any rate, it does not matter. You are famous in town now, Patience. You are famous, but not for any good thing. You are being mocked and scrutinized." He crossed his arms over his chest. "Surely you must understand why I cannot connect myself with such a woman. I will be mocked and scrutinized too."

Her throat tightened. "This is temporary. You know how people in London forget old gossip as soon as something better presents itself. Soon enough they will have something new to fill the papers with. Everyone will forget my name and my face."

"I wonder how they recognized you if you were portrayed as a monstrous creature." Lord Clitheroe stepped closer, tipping his head to one side as he examined her features. "And why were you portrayed as such at all? Mr. Cavinder must have found much to dislike when he looked at you."

She shrunk back, fighting the tears behind her eyes. "I assure you, this will all soon be forgotten."

Lord Clitheroe frowned. "I'm afraid I cannot take the risk. Society will understand why I have broken off the engagement. I am sorry, Patience, I truly am, but it is what I must do." He smoothed his fingers over his hair, offering a brief bow. "It has been a pleasure to come to know you and your family better."

Her family? The only pleasure he had was in coming to know Hattie. Patience could hardly speak or move or breathe. "Please, my lord. Please reconsider." Her face was on fire. How could she explain this to Mama? All that she had worked for was gone, torn out from beneath her by Mr. Cavinder's vengeful actions. How could he have been so cruel? Had her actions a year ago made him this cruel? Didn't he realize how he had ruined her? She choked on a breath as Lord Clitheroe continued toward the door. "Please, please stop." She took hold of his sleeve without thinking.

He shook her away, walking faster. His gaze was cold and hard as he walked out the door.

Patience collapsed on the sofa, burying her face in her hands. She threw the pillow beside her across the room. It collided with the longcase clock, setting it off-balance. The entire thing toppled over, crashing and shattering against the floor.

From the sounds in the hall, it seemed Mama was following the marquess to the door, trying to stop him from leaving. Patience stared at the shattered glass that now covered the floor. Each fragment might as well have been digging into her skin, slicing away at her dreams and puncturing the boundaries around her heart.

Mama burst into the drawing room a few minutes later, her face red. She would burst at any moment.

"You—" she pointed at Patience with an accusatory finger.

"I'm sorry, Mama!" Patience shouted as tears finally spilled down her cheeks. "I do not know how this happened. I could not stop it."

"You have ruined us. You have lost our connection to the marquess." Mama's voice was rasped and quiet, even more terrifying than it had been when she had shouted. "Your father will be even more upset than I am."

"It is not my fault." Patience shook her head fast. "It is all because of Mr. Cavinder. He did this. He has ruined us, not I."

"He would not have painted you as a monster if a monster is not what you are."

Patience's heart pounded with dread. She predicted Mama's next question before she said it.

"Did he see your scars?"

Chills ran over Patience's neck. She was silent for a long moment, sniffing back the tears that choked her. "Yes."

Mama closed her eyes, exhaling slowly. "Now it all makes sense. I told you never, ever to allow anyone to see them."

Patience wiped at her cheeks. "I-I didn't mean to. At his studio, I slipped on a paintbrush and he caught me by the sleeve." The memory poured back to her mind, making her heart sting with a fresh wave of humiliation. "My sleeve tore and he saw my arm. I never returned to his studio after that day. The portrait was still incomplete."

Mama nodded. "And once he saw the scars, he chose to

complete the portrait portraying you as a monster. I knew something horrible would happen if they were ever seen."

How many times would Patience feel betrayed in one week? Mr. Cavinder had seemed so kind. She had felt guilty for what she had done to him, when all along he had been capable of *this*. If Mama's theory was correct, then he had taken her greatest insecurity and used it to garner fame and attention toward his own artwork. He was benefitting from her misfortune. Her heart shattered like the longcase clock.

"What a disaster." Mama gritted her teeth. "Your father will not be pleased. Oh, how disappointed he will be. I do not wish to see his reaction when he learns the news." Mama paced the length of the room. "You are to associate with our family as little as possible until the height of this gossip is over. Your broken engagement will surely be published in the papers as well. You will never recover from the public shame of it, and we must do all we can to ensure you are far enough from us so as to not soil our family name even further."

"Where will I go?" Patience asked, her voice shaking with panic.

"I do not care." Mama closed her eyes as she rubbed her temples. "All I know is that I cannot bear to look upon you a moment longer. It is a burden on my nerves to be this angry. I have aged far too much in the last hour. Write to everyone you know who may be willing to harbor you for the summer, because you are not welcome here."

Patience's hand crept to her throat as she swallowed. Her heart pounded wildly. "Mama," she squeaked.

"Do not speak to me." Mama turned toward the door, drawing a deep breath before rushing into the hall and out of sight.

Patience sobbed, moving with slow steps toward the pianoforte. She sat down on the bench, too weak to stand. What had she done to deserve this? All she had done was withhold a few pounds from Mr. Cavinder because he had painted the wrong size for her portrait. Had the effects been so great that he had been driven to this cruel form of retaliation? Anger reared its head in her chest, drying her tears in an instant. There was nothing she could do to remove these misfortunes from her life. Crying would not help her cope with them. No, the only way to make them bearable would be to ensure Mr. Cavinder could no longer benefit from her humiliation.

A heart of stone was all she could afford. She had once told Mr. Cavinder that he would not want her as his enemy. No one would.

He would soon realize why.

CHAPTER THIRTEEN

 UMMER

Patience adjusted the mask on her nose, ensuring the ribbons were still tied around the back of her head. In the darkness of the evening, she was better able to slip through the crowd unnoticed, joining a group of five young ladies and their chaperones as they walked through the front doors of the assembly hall.

She did not miss the crowds of London, though Inglesbatch was not always a quiet town either. She moved as quickly as she could through the crowd of masked people as they joined the existing party inside the assembly hall. Patience had learned of the masquerade soon after her arrival in London. As luck would have it, her cousin Mary and her husband had taken pity on Patience and offered to allow her to live in their London townhouse with them for the summer. They had heard of *The Monstrous Debutante*, as nearly everyone in town had, and they found a thrill in harboring her within their walls. Patience would rather be a spectacle than have no place to live, so she had gladly accepted their invitation.

It was convenient, really, that her cousin lived in London.

Patience would be closer to Mr. Cavinder.

Mary was the one who had informed Patience of the masquerade. Her cousin had offered to attend with her as a chaperone, but Patience didn't have any interest in attending for the sake of socializing. She did not wish to present anyone with her true name and draw attention to herself. No one could know that the subject of *The Monstrous Debutante* was in London, and especially not Mr. Cavinder. She had to catch him by surprise, just as he had caught her by surprise. She had declined Mary's invitation, secretly planning to come alone instead.

Thankfully, Mary was quite involved in the gossip of London. She knew how Mr. Cavinder's two twin sisters, Emma and Isabel, had recently come out in society. She was also aware that Mr. Cavinder often accompanied them to social gatherings alongside their mother. Not only had Mr. Cavinder's painting garnered fame and attention, but he had as well. According to Mary, he had rented a town-house one street to the west of where Mary and her husband resided. At the heart of town, he had established a new studio, where he received far more clients than he had time for. His schedule was filled for the rest of the year and beyond, and he was far more wealthy than any tradesman ought to ever be.

Patience gritted her teeth as she forced her way past a rather large gentleman, holding her breath against the stench that he carried. The room was hot and filled to its capacity, leaving many of the guests flushed and covered in perspiration. The dancing had begun, which only added to the humidity of the room. Patience groaned inwardly. If only she did not have to wear long sleeves. She sympathized with the men in their thick jackets and stifling cravats. It was no wonder that they perspired more than the women with their short, puffed sleeves and low necklines.

Patience stopped when she reached the far corner. The holes in the eyes of her mask were small, but when she pressed it against her face, she managed to see quite clearly. For obvious reasons, it was beneficial for Patience to wear a mask. The problem, however, was that the masquerade would make locating Mr. Cavinder much more difficult. Finding his sisters needed to be her first task.

She caught sight of two petite young women near the refreshment table. Both had walnut brown hair, piled high atop their heads. Their dresses were different colors, but a similar style. When they turned around, their smiles were identical beneath their masks.

Patience's heart thudded. Mr. Cavinder must have been

nearby. Her gaze caught on a tall gentleman, at least two inches taller than anyone on that half of the room. His chocolate brown hair was swept neatly around his head. A solid jaw flecked with stubble, smiling lips, and a small crease in his chin showed beneath the mask. Patience watched from her shadowed corner as he walked toward the twins with two cups of water.

Patience kept her eyes on him as his mouth split into a smile. Anger bounded through her chest like a loose horse. How could he be smiling? How could his life be so perfect as a result of hers being ruined? She drew a deep breath, calming the turmoil of emotions that coursed through her veins. If she did not work quickly, she might lose her nerve.

There were many things that could harm a person's reputation, but Patience knew rumors to be the worst. Starting with the large group of women beside her, she pretended to stumble, knocking gently against the back of the nearest young lady. It would have been far more improper to simply introduce herself there without a chaperone and join their conversation, so she needed to allow a conversation to begin naturally.

"Oh, heavens, please do forgive me," Patience said. She laughed softly. "My new slippers are not as reliable as I had hoped."

The young lady stepped away from her, waving a hand. "Not to worry, no harm has been done."

Patience grimaced. "Perhaps it has. My ankle hurts quite badly. I cannot stand straight."

One of the older women in the group pressed a hand to her chest. The feathers of her turban rustled as she walked forward. "You poor thing. Come here. Take a seat." She gestured at the velvet chairs lining the wall directly behind their gathering of at least four matronly ladies and presumably their many daughters or nieces. Patience thanked the woman before sitting down just behind them all. She gave another false grimace. "Oh, yes, I have certainly twisted it, but it is nothing that requires the attention of a physician. I suppose I will simply refrain from dancing for the evening."

"What a shame." The woman sighed.

"I am relieved, actually," Patience said, raising her voice just enough so that the other young ladies in the circle would listen. "There was a certain man who asked me to dance whom I wished to avoid. Now I have an excuse not to be near him." She shuddered. "I would not wish any lady the displeasure of his company."

The other conversations among the ladies had ceased, and now they all listened, surrounding Patience's velvet chair. One young lady with raven black hair leaned forward, the pendant on her necklace swaying. "Who is it?"

Patience cast her gaze heavenward, hoping they could see her eyes through the mask. "I can hardly speak his name. He is the most vile, deceitful creature of my acquaintance."

One of the older women stepped forward. "We will

help you avoid him, not to worry. Where is your chaperone?"

"Thank you. That is a great relief, I assure you. My chaperone grew faint from the heat and stepped outside," Patience said.

"I see. Well, you must tell us who this gentleman is so we may also keep our daughters far from him."

The younger women all stared at Patience with round, eager eyes. "Do tell us," one with blonde curls said.

"Very well." Patience took a deep breath. "But he is not a gentleman at all. He is an artist."

The women gasped, leaning collectively toward Patience's chair, creating a barrier for the rest of the room. "Could it be...?"

"Mr. Cavinder," Patience said.

The woman who had helped Patience to her chair shook her head slowly, brows drawing together. "I did find his sudden fame in town rather suspicious. What has he done to give you such a low opinion of his character?"

Patience pressed a hand to her forehead, adding a flare of dramatics to her act. "I do not wish to bore you all with the story."

"You *must* tell us!" one of the ladies exclaimed.

"Oh, very well." Patience touched a hand to her heart. "But you must know how it pains me to speak of this. I will only tell the story if you all promise to spread the truth to as many people as you can. I wish for all of London to know the sort of man he truly is."

The women nodded with zeal, and Patience was certain

she could trust them to fulfill their duty. She began the story she had rehearsed many times.

"The painting that was displayed at the exhibition was a depiction of my dearest friend. She was a client of Mr. Cavinder's last year. She was far above his station, but he developed an attachment to her." Patience lowered her voice. "He was rather obsessed with her. He followed her and watched her when she was not aware. He, being a poor tradesman, should have never had any hope of securing her hand. When he proposed to her, she respectfully declined, but he persisted. He threatened to portray her as a monster for all of London to see if she did not accept him. She didn't believe his threats to be earnest, so she still declined, fearing for her own safety. He then carried out the threat, and her reputation is now ruined because of that wicked man." Patience shook her head. "My dear friend has suffered much because of him."

The women in the circle all shook their heads to match Patience, whispers of dismay escaping each one of them. "That is dreadful," the older woman said. "I found him quite amiable when I met him. How deceived I have been."

"And he is handsome," the young woman with the blonde curls said. "Why do handsome men so often lack good character?"

"Because the moment they become aware that they are extraordinarily handsome, they also become prideful and vain."

Patience had never thought that Mr. Cavinder was

vain, but he had been defensive and prideful at times. Perhaps he hadn't yet realized just how handsome he was. From where she sat on the velvet chair, she had lost his location. She couldn't see over the hats and tall turban feathers of the ladies surrounding her.

If she stood, she was confident her height would allow her to see over them.

Feigning a slight limp, she rose to her feet and steadied herself on the nearest woman's arm. "Thank you," Patience said. "I feel much better now."

With nonchalance, she swept her gaze across the room. Mr. Cavinder still stood near his sisters, but during Patience's act, they had moved closer to her side of the room.

"Is that Mr. Cavinder? The man with the blue mask?" one of the ladies asked in a hushed voice.

Patience nodded. She needed to hurry and find another group of people to spread her rumors to, and then the first step of her revenge would be complete.

"Stay here." The woman with the tall feather on her turban stood directly beside Patience. "I will ensure he does not approach you for the next dance." She withdrew her fan and began fanning her red, splotched skin. The room was growing hotter by the minute.

"You are very kind, but I—" Patience's voice lodged in her throat when she followed the woman's gaze to Mr. Cavinder. He was staring straight at Patience. Instinctively, she touched her mask, adjusting the corner. *Blast* her height. Had he recognized her because of that? She looked away as quickly as she could. Surely she was imagining things. But then, if she had recognized him with his mask, wasn't it possible that he could have recognized her? Not only was it possible, but it was likely.

There are two sorts of people you become overly aware of. Someone you love, and someone you loathe.

Mr. Cavinder had studied her for hours, transferred her image to a canvas, and then he had made it famous. She had been in his mind for a year, so how could he not have noticed her?

She dared to glance up again. His gaze was still fixed on her. He took one step in her direction.

The robust woman with the large feathered turban moved partially in front of Patience. The other women joined her, forming a wall of sorts. "Not to worry, my dear. Mr. Cavinder is no match for us. We will divert him."

Patience tried to let their reassurance calm her, but her mind raced. Being approached by Mr. Cavinder hadn't been part of her plan. Her plan had been to flee the room if she suspected he recognized her, but now she was surrounded by fierce, determined women, and Mr. Cavinder was far too close.

As he took the final steps toward them, she could see the deep brown of his eyes from behind his mask. A pang of sadness struck her heart. She had once thought those eyes to be kind, but what he had done to her had been far from it. She clung to the anger that burned around her heart, letting it consume the other feelings that arose at the sight of him, handsome and broad-shouldered. He had ruined her life, and she would not stop until she ruined his in return.

She glanced all around her. These ladies, it seemed, were now on her side.

CHAPTER FOURTEEN

There was only one woman who would wear long sleeves in the stuffy heat of a crowded London assembly room.

Lady Patience Hansford.

It hadn't only been her sleeves, but also her height and dark hair that had given away her disguise. Michael's pulse raced as he approached the place where he knew her to be hiding. He could have been a coward and remained in the opposite corner of the room, but his honor had demanded that he seek her out. The papers had been ruthless to Lady Patience since his painting had released, and there was no question that she had noticed. The exhibition had ended weeks before, but the people of London hadn't yet forgotten Lady Patience's face.

Michael certainly hadn't. Her face had been the start of a new life for his family. He had been able to provide his sisters with the ballgowns they had always dreamed of.

They had been granted entry to many events in town because of Michael's new fame as an artist. He had been working day and night to complete the many portraits he was now responsible for. His dreams were all coming true, but they were coming true at Lady Patience's expense.

He took a deep breath. How could he possibly form an apology or an explanation? And why should he? Lady Patience had never apologized for what she had done to him. For nearly a year he had lost his studio and worked tirelessly to provide a meager living for his family. There had been many days that they had hardly eaten in order to save money for their rent.

He nearly turned around. He had nothing to apologize for. The field was level now. He had simply repaid her for the atrocity she had given him.

"Is there something you are looking for, sir?" A large woman with a tall feather in her turban lifted her nose at him. She gave a smile that seemed rather false. Michael had never attended a masquerade, but from what he had heard, events such as these tended to loosen the bands on propriety. While masked, people tended to speak their minds more freely, throwing manners aside and bypassing introductions.

Michael shifted, attempting to see around her.

The woman moved into his line of sight. Both eyebrows shot up to the curls on her forehead.

"I—well, I thought I saw an old...acquaintance of mine." Where had Lady Patience gone? She was taller than all of these women. Michael blinked. There were many women in front of him, all eyes fixed on his face through their masks. His stomach flipped, unsettled by the attention. What were they staring at? One woman even appeared to be glaring at him. Another stood with her hands planted on her hips.

"You will not find her here," the woman in front said.

"I saw her just now." Michael scrunched his brow. "She wore an ivory gown with long sleeves. She is quite tall with dark hair. Have you seen her?"

"I have not."

"Are you certain?" Michael walked closer. "Her name is Lady Patience Hansford. There is a very important matter I wish to discuss with her."

Ever so slightly, the woman glanced behind her. Was that where Lady Patience was hiding? The wall of women was far too thick. How was he to break through it? And why on earth did all these women seem as though they wished to throw him out of the building?

"Lady Patience? The woman in your painting?"

Michael had never confirmed to anyone that Lady Patience had been the subject of his portrait. Each time he had been asked directly, he had denied it. Not surprisingly, the papers had made a different assumption.

When Michael did not answer, the woman spoke again. "She has already rejected you many times. Surely you must realize by now that she will not marry you, especially after what you did to her reputation."

Michael rubbed the side of his ear. Had he heard her

correctly? "Lady Patience never rejected me. I never asked her to marry me."

The two woman in front of him exchanged a glance before setting their harsh gazes on him again. "There is no sense denying it. Not only should you stay away from Lady Patience, but you ought to stay away from her friend as well. I am assuming the role of her chaperone and requesting that you seek a partner for your next dance elsewhere."

Michael was fairly certain he had never been so confused in his entire life. All he had done that evening was stay close beside Emma and Isabel to ensure they were safe.

"Lady Patience's friend? I have not been acquainted with any friend of Lady Patience's."

The woman glanced behind her again, a brief flicker of her gaze, but enough to reassure Michael that she was indeed hiding something—or someone. He gave a quick bow in departure before slipping away into the crowd. He walked quickly, concealing himself among all the other guests before circling around to the other side of the room. There, huddled behind the crowd of women, was the woman he still believed to be Lady Patience. Her hair was the same. Her long sleeves, her height, the lower half of her face. It had been a year since he had seen the real Lady Patience, not just the likeness, and the sight of her sent a string of a thousand emotions over his skin. What was she doing in London?

He needed to speak with her, but the crowd of matrons and glaring young ladies was surprisingly formidable.

Michael kept his eyes fixed on Lady Patience from his place amid the crowd, momentarily forgetting Emma and Isabel. He stood in a small space between two gentlemen, where he could see Lady Patience but she could not see him. A few minutes later, she left her refuge, walking toward another crowd of young ladies on the other side of the room.

With long strides, Michael threaded his way past the guests, cutting off Lady Patience's path just as she was passing the entrance to the assembly room.

She jumped back a step. With his closer view, he could see the combination of green and brown in her eyes, even behind the mask. It was her. Those eyes had been haunting him for the past year, and now here they were, blinking up at him with surprise.

"Pardon me," she muttered, attempting to slip past him.

"Lady Patience." Michael moved in front of her. His heart pounded furiously. "Stop."

She marched past with greater speed. "That is not my name. You are mistaken."

Michael caught his breath, not bothering to glance around to see if anyone was watching as he followed her toward the doors that led outside. "I know it is you."

She ignored him, walking even faster. He lost sight of her for a moment as she passed a tall and broad gentleman, but found her again as she slipped out the doors of the assembly room.

Forcing his way through the crowd, he pushed the door

open, stepping out into the cool evening air. It was a relief to be free of the stuffiness of the room. His gaze darted in all directions as he searched for any sign of Lady Patience's ivory gown and black mask. Around the corner of a brick pillar, he saw the edge of her hem.

With slow, quiet steps, he approached from behind the pillar. When he was within a few paces, he ran forward, circling around the pillar until he faced her. He had moved too quickly for her to react. She jumped, pressing a hand to her heart. "Who are you and why are you following me?" she asked.

Michael removed his mask, though he was entirely certain she already knew who he was. Why else would she have been running from him? She had recognized him just as quickly as he had recognized her.

"Lady Patience." Michael lifted his hands in surrender. "I only followed you because I wish to speak with you."

"I am not Patience." She spoke with her chin raised.

Michael groaned. "Devil take it, I know it is you."

She crossed her arms. "You have no proof."

Michael took a step closer, gesturing at her mask. "Allow me to see your face then, in order to prove that you are not Lady Patience."

Behind her mask, her eyes narrowed. "Why are you so eager to see my face, Mr. Cavinder? Is it so you can paint it as an even more hideous monster this time?" Her voice was cold, sending a chill over his skin.

He fell silent. There was so much to explain. How could he do a thorough job of it? There was no way to change the result of what his painting had done. By the raging fury in her eyes, he could only imagine it had done more harm than he had originally thought.

"I take it you saw the papers?" Michael asked in a quiet voice.

"Yes, I saw the papers." Her voice cracked. "I saw the papers that caused my betrothed, Lord Clitheroe, to break off our engagement three days before our wedding." She walked closer, until she stood just inches in front of him. "Those papers also induced my mother to inform me that I was no longer welcome in her home. I wrote to my cousin and traveled here to London with one intention." Her forefinger stabbed at his chest. "To ensure you regret what you have done to me."

Guilt spiraled through Michael's stomach. It was far worse than he could have imagined. He hadn't anticipated that his portrait would gain the fame that it had. If he had known how it would ruin Lady Patience, he would have never submitted it, no matter how tempting it was. He was not a vengeful person, but it was obvious that Lady Patience was.

"Do you regret what *you* did to *me*?" Michael asked. "Or have you even considered what the consequences of your actions might have been?"

Lady Patience's lips pressed together, and her nostrils flared. "I do not understand how my refusal of one portrait could have made me deserving of such retaliation."

"Do you think I anticipated this?" Michael shook his head. "I assure you, these results were not my intention.

My father was dying. When I secured you as a client, I was hopeful, but when I secured Lord Clitheroe, I knew it was my best opportunity to establish a business that could provide for my mother and sisters. Because you encouraged the marquess to cancel his appointment with me, the reputation of my business suffered. For nearly a year, I struggled to feed my family. I was forced to close my father's studio. My anger led me to alter your portrait, but only as an expression of my creativity and emotions. I never meant to publicize it, not until my father expressed his dying wish that I submit the piece to the exhibition. I didn't expect it to be accepted, nor did I expect the fame it has garnered." He looked straight into her eyes to ensure he was not misunderstood. "No matter how you harmed me, Lady Patience, I never wished to see you harmed. This was not an act of revenge."

A soft breeze passed between them, rustling the curls on Lady Patience's brow. She stared at him for several seconds, fists curled at her sides. "Then why did you paint me as a monster? You are the only one who has ever seen the scars on my arm." Her voice hardened. "You cannot pretend that your actions in exploiting my weaknesses were not vengeful."

Michael frowned, shaking his head. The memory of Lady Patience, shaking and embarrassed, flashed through his mind. How had she managed to hide her scars from everyone but him? He had never learned how she procured them, but the subject seemed far too sensitive to breach. "I did not paint you as a monster because of your arms." He emphasized his words.

Her glare faltered. "You didn't?"

"*No*, of course not." Michael's heart stung. Had she really believed that he would make such a mockery of her physical ailment? He remembered that she hadn't yet seen the portrait. All she knew from the papers was that she was painted 'as a monster.' In her mind, that could have meant he had displayed the scars on her arms that she was so ashamed of.

"Then why?" Her voice was weak.

"It was because of your actions." He rubbed one side of his face. "I was hurt by what you did the day you left my studio for the last time. I was angry. I had wanted to believe you were good and kind, but after you left that day, I could no longer believe that. In that moment, you seemed very much like a monster in disguise."

In the moonlight, Lady Patience's skin glowed and her eyes flashed with anger. She looked regal and beautiful and dangerous, all at once. "It seems I was once the cause of your ruin, and you were the cause of mine. Are we both monsters, then?"

The question hung heavy between them. His eyes locked with hers. He wished he could go back in time and destroy the portrait of Lady Patience before he had ever submitted it. What had he been thinking? He had been thinking of his father and his family, but not of Lady Patience. Perhaps he was a monster in his own right. "Either we are both monsters," Michael began, "or we are both ordinary people who have made terrible mistakes. People who have been selfish and unkind, perhaps too unforgiving. Which would you prefer to believe?"

Lady Patience's posture relaxed slightly, but her eyes remained fixed on his. With her dark, dramatic brows hidden behind her mask, her expression was more difficult to read. As he watched her, he could almost see the layers of her pride unfolding, and he observed the great effort that each layer took to peel away. "I would believe the latter." She took a deep breath. "But I would also believe that your deeds have been worse than mine. You are now successful. You have risen above your circumstances. You are famous in London for your talent and success, and I—" She looked down at the ground. "I will never recover from this."

A fresh wave of guilt collided against his heart. "I was once certain that I would never recover. Though I do regret the actions which led me to where I am today, I am grateful that my family no longer starves. You will recover."

"You do not understand." Her gaze cut through him. "My family has abandoned me. They do not wish to see me or associate with me. News of my broken engagement with the marquess has already begun circulating. I am not being unreasonable when I say that my life will never be the same again." The anger that threaded through her words was still directed at Michael. The blame was still there, and he deserved all of it.

"I know my words will not suffice, but I wish to offer my most sincere apology. I will destroy the portrait. I will do all I can to reverse the effect it has had on your reputation."

Her head gave one concise shake. "No."

Michael raised his eyebrows. "No?"

Lady Patience planted her hands on her hips, lifting her chin. "You will not destroy the portrait until I've seen it."

CHAPTER FIFTEEN

*I*t was natural to assume that a London art studio would be more spacious than one in Inglesbatch, but even with that assumption, Patience was shocked by the grandeur of Mr. Cavinder's new studio. She had never thought she would venture to call an art studio *grand*, but this one was. The floor appeared to have been newly installed, large windows letting in light from outside. Though the bustle of people and horses could be heard from outside, there was a certain peacefulness within the walls of the studio that calmed the turmoil in Patience's stomach. Partially completed paintings on stretched canvases were laid about the room. A ladder, many stools, and short tables filled the other areas of the space. Shelves were filled with supplies, and a closet of sorts sat in the back corner of the room.

Patience stood near the front door, frozen in place as

Mr. Cavinder stepped out from inside the closet, a wrapped canvas in hand. It was the size she had been anticipating.

Three-quarters of a yard to be precise.

The size that had caused her to burst out in a ridiculous fit of emotions. How different her life would have been if she had simply maintained her composure. She rubbed her arms, overcome with a sudden chill.

Mr. Cavinder closed the closet door behind him, tugging it shut with what appeared to be a great deal of effort. It closed with a thud, hinges creaking. When he turned to face her, his mouth was a firm line. "I did have it hidden in the back of the closet for a reason. I hope you know I took it back from the exhibition as soon as I could."

Patience swallowed, watching each step he took toward her with misgiving. Ever since he had discovered her at the masquerade the night before, she had been cautious. The anger in her heart begged her to hate him, but she couldn't manage it, not when her own shame battled for dominance. Mr. Cavinder had ruined her life, but she had first ruined his. He was still a better person that she was. He hadn't painted this monstrous portrait for revenge, yet she had come to London to spread terrible rumors about him. She had been vengeful when he had been remorseful.

Her heart thudded as the corner of the portrait came uncovered. She met Mr. Cavinder's gaze, and her heart thudded again. She had forgotten just how handsome he was. In the dim evening light at the masquerade she hadn't had as clear a view as the one she had now. His warm brown eyes launched a slew of emotions straight into her chest. How many emotions could be associated with one man? Was it possible to dislike a man and find him unjustly attractive at the same time?

"My lady," he said in a quiet voice, "before I show you this portrait, I would like you to know that this does not reflect my opinion of you. It reflects a few hours of frustration, during which I unleashed my creativity." He gave a weak smile. "I hope you understand."

She crossed her arms. "If I had any creativity to unleash, I wonder how I would portray you."

"I wonder the same thing." Mr. Cavinder's smile grew, just a twitch of his lips. "I daresay I would look like a sea monster. Perhaps a mythical troll."

Patience studied his face. She would have never told him, but she could not imagine him as any menacing creature. With his thick brown hair and chocolate brown eyes, he could be a puppy before he could be anything else. "Of those two options, I'm certain you would be the troll."

"I am flattered, thank you." Mr. Cavinder's smiling eyes met hers, cautious and slow, as if he were testing her willingness to accept any teasing. If Mama were here, she would tell her not to be alone at this studio with Mr. Cavinder at all, and certainly not to be conversing with him so casually. Despite his fame and prestige as an artist, he was still, well, an artist. He was not a gentleman, and therefore Mama would disapprove. The only way Mama would ever approve of her again would be if she somehow managed to become engaged to a titled gentleman again.

Given her reputation, the odds of that were nearly impossible. That was why she had been in the process of giving up. Ever since arriving in London she had been schooling herself into giving up on her dreams. It had been more difficult than she had anticipated. To be loved and accepted by her parents, to be as admired as Hattie—these had been her dreams for so long. Their ties were buried underneath her skin. They had become so much a part of her that they were difficult to remove.

She drew a deep breath. "Show me the painting."

Mr. Cavinder hesitated before removing the covering on the canvas, letting it slip to the floor at his feet.

Patience walked closer to the piece, stomach twisting with dread. It was certainly still recognizable as her. She hadn't expected one half of her face to still be unchanged from when he had first shown her the painting. The lines blended seamlessly as her face transformed to a monster's on the opposite side. The ear, fangs, horn, and sunken skin sent a chill over the back of her neck. Perhaps if it hadn't been a picture of her, she would have found it as hauntingly breathtaking as the rest of society did. It was certainly *haunting.*

She looked down at the floor, feeling suddenly nauseated. "This is how all of London knows me now." The reality sank into her bones. "This is how you saw me."

"I believe it was the message that struck people so deeply," Mr. Cavinder said, stooping down to cover the portrait again. "They were reminded how deceiving beauty can be at times." His eyes flickered to her face. "They were reminded of their own masks, and of the masks worn by all the people around them. I daresay no one walks bare-faced. Especially not in London."

Patience touched one side of her face, rubbing the smooth skin on her cheek. Immediately her thoughts traveled to Hattie. If her beauty was gone, what would remain? So many admired her and flocked to her simply because she was beautiful. Even their parents failed to see who she truly was. They had never seen the truth about Hattie. Patience hadn't even seen it—not completely—until she had seen her with Lord Clitheroe behind the tree. She wore her mask well. Beneath it, Patience was certain a formidable monster lurked, waiting to destroy everything in its path.

Had Patience become the same?

The thought persisted, echoing in her mind until she could scarcely hear anything else. Terror gripped her heart.

She did *not* wish to be like Hattie.

Mr. Cavinder stepped closer, holding the covered portrait between them. "You are not a monster, Lady Patience." The warmth in his eyes made her heart give a strange, unexpected leap.

"I did a terrible thing to you." It was the first time she had admitted it, and the confession lifted a burden from her shoulders. She no longer hated him. She was beginning to understand him a little. Bitterness was heavy, and the only way to ease the weight was to forgive and move forward. In comparison to Hattie's betrayal, Mr. Cavinder's actions were insignificant.

"And I did a terrible thing to you." Mr. Cavinder ran a

hand over his hair, glancing up at her from under his lashes. "Shall we consider both our debts repaid?"

She bit her lip, shifting her gaze away from him. "Well —I'm afraid I already did begin my revenge at the masquerade."

"Your revenge?" Without even looking, she could predict Mr. Cavinder's expression. Eyebrows raised, eyes filled with curiosity.

"The women you saw surrounding me...well, I told them something about you that was not entirely true." Her face grew hot. She shooed the sensation away, willing her cheeks to cool. How could she explain the rumor to him? In the story, he had been obsessed with her, proposing multiple times and being rejected. She had turned him into a vengeful, bitter madman before she had known that he was far more innocent than that. Not entirely innocent, but only as innocent as her.

"What did you tell them?" Mr. Cavinder tipped his head to one side, setting the portrait on the floor.

"You will likely hear the story eventually. Though once it has passed through a number of ears and mouths, it will likely have been transformed into a different story entirely." She avoided his gaze, shifting her weight from one boot to the other.

He eyed her with suspicion. "Did you tell them I am secretly a troll?"

"No." She scoffed, breathless at the wide smile he was giving her. Was he not concerned over the rumors she had started? Didn't he fear for his reputation? He didn't seem fazed at all. Simply curious.

"Then what did you tell them? I did wonder why they all seemed inclined to throw me out the assembly room window."

Patience stifled the laugh that rose in her chest, thankfully before Mr. Cavinder could hear it. She couldn't have him knowing that she found any part of his words or expression amusing. She felt vulnerable in his presence. He had seen her at her worst, including the scars on her arm. Her defenses were weakened. She was not accustomed to feeling at ease around a gentleman. Well, Mr. Cavinder was not a gentleman. He was a plain *man*. Not a plain man, though. A very handsome one. Her scattered thoughts made her face grow hot again. He was still waiting for her explanation about the rumors.

"I told them that I was Lady Patience's 'friend,' and that the reason you painted the portrait was because you had proposed to her many times and been rejected. Because of your bitterness, you sought revenge by exploiting her face as *The Monstrous Debutante,* intentionally ruining her reputation." Patience wished she could cover her own face. She had just pointed out her moral inferiority to Mr. Cavinder. She *was* vengeful and he was not.

He was silent for a long moment before he tipped his head back with a laugh. She stared at him, blinking in surprise.

"There is one flaw in your story." He picked up the portrait, carrying it back to the closet at the back of his studio. He tugged hard on the door, pulling three times before it jerked open. He set the portrait inside, then glanced back at her. "Why on earth would your friend Lady Patience have rejected me?"

The day before, Patience would have been able to think of hundreds of reasons, but staring at his broad shoulders and charming smile made her mind go rather blank. Patience crossed her arms across her chest. "Perhaps she thought you to be a little too prideful."

His mouth quirked upward. "A weakness of mine, to be sure."

Patience tapped her fingertips together, ignoring the flutter in her stomach at his smile. It took far more courage than she possessed to admit her own weaknesses. Mr. Cavinder's willingness to admit his almost made up for his pride. Almost. She caught sight of his amused grin as he closed the closet door.

Her eyes wandered the shop one last time. She needed to leave. Being there reminded her of all the hours she had spent at his shop in Inglesbatch, and so did the uncalled for feelings stirring around her heart. Her gaze caught on a painting in the far corner of the room, uncovered and glistening, as if some of the paint had not yet dried. It was still in progress, it seemed. While Mr. Cavinder's back was turned, she walked toward it.

He truly was a talented artist. He deserved the fame he had achieved, if only for that reason. The piece depicted a man, one hand outstretched in front of him toward a beam of light, one behind him toward darkness. At the end of the hand cloaked in darkness was a woman, clutching his fingers as she ascended a slope behind him. She seemed as though she were about to slip away and fall down the slope, just the tips of her fingers still touching his. The man's head was turned toward her, his eyes settled on her with terror. Many of the details had not yet been completed, but the sketch was there, and even in its incomplete state it captivated her.

"Do you like it?" Mr. Cavinder's voice behind her made her jump.

She caught her breath, still hesitant to admit any admiration for his work. She finally managed one small word. "Yes."

He stepped up beside her. "I plan to submit this to the next exhibition. I have always been fascinated by Orpheus and Eurydice."

Patience had been taught mythology by her governess, and now that Mr. Cavinder mentioned Orpheus, the painting struck her even deeper. If she recalled correctly, in the myth, Orpheus and Eurydice were madly in love when Eurydice was bitten by a serpent and died. Orpheus journeyed to the land of Hades to rescue her, granted access and escape only because of his enchanting musical talent. He was allowed to bring Eurydice back to the land of the living only if he promised not to look back at her. He had to trust that she was behind him, even when he could not hear her shadow.

Mr. Cavinder's voice was low and thoughtful as he joined her in studying the piece. "This painting depicts the precise moment of the worst mistake Orpheus ever made. Seconds before reaching the light, he was too curious, and he lacked trust that Eurydice could transform from shadow to light. He was impatient, and then he lost her forever."

Patience glanced at Mr. Cavinder, meeting his gaze. "The myth has always vexed me. Why could Orpheus not have been a little more patient?"

Amusement crossed his features. "As I recall, patience is not one of your virtues either."

She scowled at him before relenting. He had just admitted to his pride, so she ought to admit to her impatience. "Yes, I suppose I might have done the same thing."

With morning light filtering through the windows and pulling warm tones from Mr. Cavinder's eyes, he gave another of his heart-stopping smiles. Patience immediately looked down at the floor, cursing her heart for reacting. She started walking away, tying the ribbons on her bonnet. "Very well. Now that I have seen *The Monstrous Debutante*, you may destroy her."

"I will."

She stopped by the front door, giving a brief nod in departure. "Good day, Mr. Cavinder."

She didn't wait for him to bid his own farewell. She marched out into the street, pulling the wide brim of her poke bonnet lower over her eyes. It was the only way she could walk around town without risking being recognized. If she were seen outside of Mr. Cavinder's studio, the rumors would become even worse.

The studio door opened behind her. "My lady, wait." It was Mr. Cavinder's voice.

She glanced back, checking to ensure no one had heard him say her name. The streets were crowded and filled with the sounds of creaking carriage wheels, shouting, and horse hooves on the cobblestones.

Mr. Cavinder stood with his head and shoulders leaning out the studio door. "Would you like to join my family for dinner one evening this week? Thursday, perhaps?"

Patience froze. She hadn't planned on making any social calls, and certainly not with the family of the man she had presumed to be her enemy. She had taken certain liberties with her efforts to preserve her reputation, such as attending a masquerade alone. Attending dinner alone would be improper as well, but Mr. Cavinder's cajoling smile was difficult to refuse. Her heart betrayed her, and before she knew it, one blasted word had slipped from her mouth.

"Yes."

After arranging the details, Patience walked away, left to wonder *what* exactly had come over her. Mr. Cavinder with his kind eyes and half-rolled shirtsleeves was an intelligent guess. All her resolve to hate him had fled from her heart as quickly as she had fled from his studio.

Even more concerning was the realization that she was now looking forward to Thursday.

CHAPTER SIXTEEN

"She frightens me a little," Emma said in a whisper as she and Isabel waited by the drawing room window for Lady Patience's arrival. "Michael, why did you invite her?"

"Yes, why *did* you invite her?" Isabel turned away from the window, curls swaying.

Michael straightened his cravat, shrugging one shoulder.

"Are you in love with her?" Emma asked in an accusatory voice.

"No." Michael scoffed, though the question made him a little too defensive. "You two are being ridiculous. I invited her because she needs friends."

The twins exchanged a wary glance. "Does she want friends?"

"I'm not certain." That was the question Michael had been battling with. There was much he still did not know about Lady Patience, but he knew she was a human, not a monster, and humans did not often thrive when they were alone. Because of his portrait, Lady Patience had been banished from her home, and it ached his heart to know that it was all his fault. "Whether she wants friends or not, we must all treat her with kindness. The misfortunes she suffers now have come at my hand, so it is our responsibility to help her in any way that we are able."

Mother stood near Michael, listening to the conversation. She nodded her approval. "Not to worry, we will be kind to Lady Patience. Won't we?" She eyed the twins, who each gave a reluctant nod.

"She still does frighten me," Emma mumbled.

"You are not alone. She frightens me a little too," Michael said. He chuckled under his breath. It was embarrassing to confess, but it was true. Underneath her bristled exterior though, Michael suspected Lady Patience was hiding something. He couldn't believe that she was naturally so coarse. She had built those walls and thorns herself for a reason he didn't yet know, but was determined to discover.

Isabel gasped. "She's here!" Then she ducked below the windowsill, crawling out of sight before standing at the opposite corner of the room.

Michael caught sight of her blue pelisse out the window, complete with the three brass buttons down the back. The image gave rise to the memory of when he had first seen her at the cricket match in that same jacket. She had worn it in the middle of summer, just as she did now.

"Does she wear long sleeves to cover the scars on her arms?" Emma asked. Michael had forgotten that his sisters had also witnessed Lady Patience's torn sleeve that day in his studio.

"I suppose so," Michael said. "But we must not speak of it around her. Do you understand?"

They nodded. "I wouldn't dare," Isabel said.

"She might bite me if I did," Emma added.

Michael hid his smile as he turned away from the window. Less than a minute passed before Lady Patience joined them in the drawing room of the townhouse. As she passed through the doorway, a hush fell over the room. Her fingers were interlocked in front of her, shoulders pushed back and chin high. Michael's gaze hovered over her face. He knew it so well, yet he was still surprised by her beauty each time he saw her. The green in her eyes was more prominent tonight, brought out by the blue of her pelisse. Her dark lashes swept down, casting shadows over her cheeks. When her gaze found his, it flickered to the floor.

Michael walked forward, tipping his head down to look at her. His objective was obtained when she lifted her eyes from the floor and looked up at him. "Welcome to our home, my lady." He smiled, hoping to erase the unease in her features. "You have met my sisters, Emma and Isabel, and this is my mother, Mrs. Cavinder." He waved her forward. "Mother, meet Lady Patience Hansford."

The two exchanged bows of greeting. As the daughter of an earl, anyone would have been surprised to see Lady Patience willing to dine with their family, but she seemed to have gained a little humility since he had last known her the year before. She also seemed more weary, and perhaps a little broken.

"It is a pleasure to finally meet you, my lady," Mother said. "I am so grateful that Michael invited you here."

"I am grateful to have been invited," Lady Patience said. Her face was stoic.

As they began removing to the dining room, Michael stopped beside Lady Patience, extending his arm. She took it slowly, keeping her gaze fixed forward. Her fingers wrapped around his elbow. "I should have asked what your favorite meal is," Michael said, leaning slightly toward her ear. She smelled of roses. He snapped his posture back, keeping his mind focused. "I hope you like mutton."

"I do not."

Michael's chest deflated, but a surge of irritation followed the disappointment. She could have at least pretended she liked it. Lady Patience was nothing if not honest. Well, aside from the rumors she had spread about him at the ball.

A slight twitch at the corner of her mouth made him freeze. After several seconds of his frustrated silence, she looked at him sidelong. "In truth, it is my favorite."

He let out a laugh of disbelief. He hadn't thought her capable of teasing. He looked down at her as they walked, struggling to understand the variance in her behavior. His gaze caught on the necklace at her chest. It was engraved at the edges with a pearl embedded at the center. A small piece of lilac amethyst hung by a threadlike chain from the larger pendant. The unique design flooded his mind with recognition.

It was the necklace Mother had sold.

He had no doubt.

He stared at it for a long moment, noting once again the engravings on the sides. He stopped walking, too shocked to move.

He tore his gaze away from the pendant after several more seconds, raising his attention to Lady Patience's face.

She was glaring at him.

His face warmed as he realized how his attentions must have appeared. The location of her necklace was a place his eyes should not have lingered so long. "Your necklace," he blurted. He nearly looked at it again, but was now far too embarrassed to lower his gaze. "Where did you find it?"

Her scowl persisted as she glanced down at the pendant, covering it with one hand. "My mother purchased it for me in Inglesbatch."

"Did she purchase it previously owned?"

Lady Patience's brow furrowed. "I believe so."

Michael glanced at Mother, Emma, and Isabel, who had all entered the dining room up ahead. He shook his head with disbelief before turning back toward Lady Patience. "This necklace belonged to my mother. She sold it so I would have enough money to purchase the roll of canvas I used for your portrait more than one year ago."

Lady Patience uncovered the pendant, eyes wide with wonder. "Are you certain it was hers?"

"Yes. I have never seen a pendant like it before."

Lady Patience fell silent, rubbing the pearl between her fingers.

"That is a very odd coincidence," Michael said, meeting her gaze.

She nodded, her voice distant. "Indeed."

Michael observed as she fiddled with the pendant at her neck for the first few minutes of dinner. She might have been doing it unintentionally, but her actions drew more attention to it than if she had left it alone. Michael watched the precise moment Mother recognized the necklace. She was between spoonfuls of soup, the utensil hovering near her mouth as her eyes settled on the pendant. She covered her surprise well, continuing to eat her soup after just a moment's hesitation.

The irony of the situation would not leave Michael's mind. Of all that Lady Patience had taken from him the year before, she had also taken his mother's necklace with her. And now, despite all that she had lost, she still had that one piece of their family. It connected Lady Patience to them, as if fate had known their paths would cross again.

Michael often thought too deeply for his own good, but he couldn't help but think of his father. The man had been fond of irony. Perhaps this was all his doing.

Michael glanced heavenward, making sure his father knew of his suspicions.

As the meal carried on, Lady Patience seemed to grow more comfortable. Mother was gracious and kind, avoiding sensitive topics and subjects, focusing instead on conversations that were not personal, asking Lady Patience for advice on the current fashion trends for Emma and Isabel as well as the best social events to attend in town. His sisters had only been included in so many events because of Michael's fame from the exhibition. He feared that it would not last forever. People would soon remember that Emma and Isabel were not the daughters of a gentleman.

From across the table, Michael watched Lady Patience's stoic expression relax, leaving small gaps of vulnerability. Each time she smiled, Michael's heart stalled. She glanced at him periodically, as if to ensure he wasn't noticing these cracks in her stone walls. Unfortunately for her, he had noticed each and every one.

In the drawing room, Emma requested that they play charades. Lady Patience did not play, but simply watched. Michael was certain he made a fool of himself as he acted far too enthusiastically as a jaguar in order for he and his mother's team to win. Lady Patience's laugh made it worth the embarrassment. He had never heard her laugh, but even as quiet and stifled as it was, he was grateful to have earned it.

Shortly after the game ended, Lady Patience stood. "I must be going. I thank you for your hospitality this evening." She turned to Mother with a small smile.

"It has been our pleasure, Lady Patience," Mother said. "If you feel so inclined, please join us for tea at two o'clock tomorrow afternoon."

Lady Patience hesitated before giving a faint nod. Another smile pulled on her lips. "Thank you."

Her eyes grazed over Michael before she bowed in his

direction, starting toward the door. He followed her out into the entry hall. Very few candles were lit there, leaving just a faint glow by which to see. Flickering shadows came and went with the breeze from the open door.

"Thank you for coming," Michael said. "Did you enjoy the evening?"

Lady Patience tied her bonnet, turning to face him. Her movements were slow and careful. "I did."

"I'm glad to hear it." He gave a soft smile. "You are welcome here anytime you wish. Do you—do you like living with your cousin?"

Lady Patience looked down at her gloves, tugging at each fingertip. "She and her husband have been very generous taking me in."

That did not answer his question, but by the sadness in her eyes, he could guess at the answer. "I assume you are comfortable there for the time being, but you must also feel uncertain about your future?"

Her lips pressed together. "My cousin won't wish to harbor me forever. I still have to hide my face in London so I am not recognized."

"You don't have to hide anything here." He gestured all around him at the house. "Nothing at all, and you are welcome anytime you wish. I know it cannot mend what I have done, but I wish to do all I can to ensure you are safe and comfortable."

Lady Patience's brow twitched, and she drew an audible breath. As she exhaled, her hand rose to the pendant at her neck. "Will you return this to your mother for me?" her voice was abrupt.

Michael studied the determination in her features. "It is yours now. You don't need to return it to her."

"I want to." She lifted her arms and began working at the clasp behind her neck. With her thick gloves, she struggled for several seconds.

He took a cautious step forward, touching her elbow.

Her arms lowered slowly to her sides, and her gaze followed him as he stepped behind her. A few curls fell over the slope of the back of her neck. He brushed them aside, ignoring the hammering of his pulse as his fingers grazed her skin. He needed to stop allowing himself to be so affected by her. Working quickly, he unclasped the necklace, letting it fall into Lady Patience's palms.

She turned to face him, a slight flush on her cheeks, visible even in the faint light. "Mr. Cavinder—" she paused, thrusting the necklace into his hand. "I-I *am* sorry for what I did." The words seemed to almost cause her physical pain from the humility that they required.

Before he could respond, she whirled around and walked out the door.

CHAPTER SEVENTEEN

Autumn, 1817

Every time Patience left her cousin Mary's house, she set her poke bonnet low on her forehead, keeping her eyes shaded and hidden from view. She had expected her time in London to be filled with turmoil and a lack of structure, but she had established something of a routine over the months that she had spent in town.

In the mornings, she ate breakfast with Mary. She then went to her room to read and watch the birds in the trees behind the house. Three days out of each week, she watched the clock, eagerly awaiting the hour when she could take her ride to the Cavinders' and take tea with Mrs. Cavinder, Emma, and Isabel in the quaint, simple drawing room of their townhouse.

Over the last few months, Mrs. Cavinder had enlisted Patience's assistance in training her daughters in dancing, manners, and fashion so they would have a chance at catching the eye of a gentleman—or at least a wealthy tradesman. Mrs. Cavinder's mothering methods were much different than that of Patience's mother. She encouraged her daughters and never pointed out a single flaw in their appearances or conduct. She praised them and celebrated with them when they managed to complete a dance without error. She explained that the reason they were to seek husbands was not for prestige or recognition. She told them that all she wished for them was that they were happy, comfortable, and loved.

Two of those words, *happy* and *loved*, had embedded themselves in Patience's chest, burrowing close to her heart. As she considered the ambitions that she had been taught to have throughout her entire life, she could not recall ever hearing those two words. But despite never hearing them, she realized that those two things had still always been her ambitions.

But to be happy, she had to be loved.

To be loved, she had to be approved of.

To be approved of…she had to be flawless and beautiful and married to a man with a title.

The contrast between the Cavinder family and her own had struck her. For Emma and Isabel to be loved by their mother, it seemed all they had to do was exist. No matter how hard Patience tried, she couldn't help but envy them.

There was little Patience wouldn't give for that sort of love —the sort of love that persisted beyond mistakes, flaws, and tribulation. The sort of love that is unbreakable. If she could ever be loved simply for existing, perhaps she would finally be happy. She hadn't known that sort of love was real, but she saw it displayed again and again as Mrs. Cavinder interacted with her daughters and also with her son.

Mr. Cavinder spent his days in his studio, but sometimes he made it home just a few minutes before Patience left the drawing room after tea. If he ever made it back before she left, he insisted that she stay for dinner. She had developed the strength to say no to his mother's kind offerings, but she hadn't yet learned how to say no to Mr. Cavinder. Though she knew it wasn't wise, sometimes she lingered a little longer after tea in the hopes that he would arrive before she left.

She didn't dare examine her heart, but she knew in her bones that if she did, she would find that it was beginning to feel things it shouldn't. Hope had injured her far too many times to ever trust it again. Each time she entertained the thought of Mr. Cavinder having any feelings for her, she shunned the idea as quickly as it came. There were many reasons why she could not allow such thoughts into her mind. Or her heart for that matter. He had seen the scars on her arms. He had experienced her bitterness and unkindness. Her actions could never be undone, no matter how much she wished it now.

He was entirely too good for her.

After she had come to London in pursuit of revenge, he had opened his home to her. He had met her malice with kindness and introduced her to his family.

It was a debt she could never repay.

Her entire life, she had felt like a burden everywhere she went. She had never felt good enough beneath the lofty expectations of her parents and the precedence of Hattie. She never would have imagined that one day she would be yearning to be good enough for the attention of a humble painter.

Perhaps she was too cold toward him. It was a habit of hers to conceal her true emotions by being aloof. In her experience, it was the only way to protect herself. If her actions made her feelings known, she could not afford a rejection from Mr. Cavinder. It would break what remained of her heart.

She told herself that it was goodwill and honor that had induced him to treat her so kindly, not affection. The sooner she recognized that, the better. At any rate, her time in London was measured. The weather was growing colder. The summer was over. Eventually her family would have to invite her home again and she would leave the Cavinders behind. She refused to believe that her parents had abandoned her forever, even though she hadn't received a single letter from them during her time in London. Each of the letters she sent to Briarwood failed to receive a reply.

Not a single word.

Were they alive and well? Did they care if she was? The more time that passed, the more abandoned she felt. Without the Cavinders, she didn't know what she would have done. They had saved her.

One morning, Emma and Isabel invited Patience to collect leaves with them. She had never engaged in such a strange activity, but she agreed. The leaves had begun changing color, spiraling down to the earth in a graceful and final descent. The bright ambers, saffrons, and burnt siennas dotted the ground beneath the trees along their street.

Patience collected all the red ones she could find, piling them on her leather glove. She wore her blue pelisse, wishing for a color more suitable to autumn. The money her parents had sent her away with was more than enough to provide herself with a new pelisse, but she didn't wish to be wasteful. She didn't know how long she would only have that money to live on.

"Michael!" Emma waved across the street.

Patience's heart leaped as she followed Emma's gaze. Mr. Cavinder was striding toward them, a broad smile on his face. He waved, his eyes settling on Patience as he stopped in front of them. He lowered his head in greeting. "My lady."

She did the same, suddenly conscious of how red her nose must have appeared in the cold. "Mr. Cavinder."

"I was on my way home," he said. "My client this afternoon postponed his appointment."

"How fortunate," Patience said. "You may now join us in collecting leaves."

He dipped his chin, laughing. "I will be glad to."

Emma and Isabel walked ahead, choosing the best leaves for themselves along the side of the street. Patience slowed her pace, her stomach tying itself in knots. Mr. Cavinder walked beside her. She could hardly remember the last time they had been able to speak privately. He had been spending so many hours in his studio, and when he did return home while she was there, so were the other members of his family.

"May I see what you have collected so far?" Mr. Cavinder asked, holding out his hand. Patience set the leaves in his palm, noting the streaks of paint on his skin and fingernails. She smiled to herself.

He examined each leaf closely, holding them up to his eyes. She took the opportunity to study his features without being noticed. Her heart pounded a little faster when his smile brought creases to the corners of his eyes. When his eyes turned back to her, she could see her reflection against the warm brown tones. "These are all the same color," he said in a baffled voice.

"I know." She took the leaves back, spreading them like a hand of cards. "I like the red ones best."

His smile tipped sideways as he looked down at her. She didn't mind being so tall when she was standing near Mr. Cavinder. He was still a few inches taller than her, and she was able to have a much closer view of his handsome face than many other women would have when standing beside him. The idea of other women standing so close to him stabbed her with a pang of envy. She pushed it away, focusing on the leaves instead.

"The colors of autumn are all meant to complement one another," Mr. Cavinder said. "I think you ought to add some other hues to your collection if it is to be complete." As he gestured at the ground with his paint-streaked hands, he was far too endearing. If only she could view the world as an artist viewed it. The passion behind his words was infectious.

"Sir, I think one's satisfaction with their collection of leaves is up to their own opinion." She cast him a sidelong glance, bending to pick up another red leaf.

He stared at her, crossing his arms. Just when she thought he would scold her for choosing the red leaf, he surprised her. "You mustn't call me sir. Call me Michael. I think we have been friends long enough."

The word *friends* rattled through Patience's mind. On one hand, she was flattered that he had called her his friend. On the other, she was disappointed. "But lest you forget, we were enemies long before we were ever friends."

He laughed. "I suppose that is true. One would never address their enemy so informally."

"Never." Patience gave a shy smile. "I suppose it is time that I break the habit of addressing you as I would an enemy."

"I will do the same." Mr. Cavinder—*Michael*—stopped beneath a tree. "Though I do hesitate to address you as Patience. Shall I call you Impatience instead?"

She crossed her arms, crushing her collection of leaves. "I was only impatient during the hours I had to sit while you painted my portrait. Of late I have been very patient, if you must know."

"Have you?" Michael raised one eyebrow. "What is it you have been so patiently waiting for?"

She drew a deep breath, pressing her lips together. The things that she had been growing impatient about were things she would never, ever tell him. What had she been waiting for, exactly? Some indication that Michael cared for her as more than an acquaintance, or even a friend? She did not like waiting for things that would likely never come. If she made a habit of it, then she would spend her entire life in the throes of disappointment.

"That leaf." She pointed above his head. "I have been waiting for you to move so I can pluck that leaf for my collection." A single red leaf hovered on a branch above Michael's head. She hadn't noticed it until that precise moment, but he didn't need to know that.

Michael threw her a suspicious look before stepping aside. Patience marched forward, rising on her toes to reach for the leaf. From the corner of her eye, she saw him turn to face the tree, watching as she struggled to reach it. From where she stood, she was nearly touching Michael's arm. She could feel both his gaze and the warmth of his breath as he laughed in the cold autumn air. When he spoke, his voice came from behind, close to her ear. "You almost have it."

"Well, are you going to help me or simply watch me

struggle?" Patience asked. Her own laugh escaped, but it came out breathless when she felt Mr. Cavinder's hand press against her lower back. He must have thought he was steadying her, but his touch had the opposite effect. Her balance faltered on her toes. Her heart pounded as his hands moved to grip each side of her waist.

"On the count of three, jump," he said. "I'll lift you up to the leaf."

Patience doubted her shaking legs were even capable of jumping, but she would try, if only to ensure that Michael kept his hands precisely where they were, flush against her waist.

"One, two, three!" His grip tightened as he hoisted her up.

She snatched the leaf, letting out a small shriek as she fell back down to the ground. Michael slowed her descent, laughing into her hair as she stumbled back against him. Her skin rushed with warmth as she turned around to show him her prize.

His hands slid away from her waist, and when she faced him, his mouth was pulled into a broad smile. When she realized how close she still stood to him, she staggered back a step. Her back met the rough bark of the tree trunk. She had no where to go, and Michael didn't seem intent to step aside. The smile on his face softened, and he hardly looked at the leaf she had extended toward him. His attentions were otherwise engaged.

His eyes traced over her face as the last remnants of his laughter faded. Patience was still catching her breath, smiling up at him because she couldn't stop herself. Her heart pounded hard enough to prove that she did still have a heart, and that it was in immense danger of being stolen. Michael lifted his fingers to her face, brushing a loose curl away from her eyebrow. She held her breath, unwilling to interrupt whatever it was that Michael was doing. Her skin tingled under his touch, awakening the abandoned emotions in the pit of her stomach. She was not certain she could have inhaled even if she tried.

"Patience—" he began in a soft voice. He paused, his jaw tightening as he looked down at the ground. "I have been meaning to thank you for befriending my sisters. They have come to adore you. My mother cares for you more than you realize." He lowered his hand from her face, kicking at a leaf near his boot. His brows drew together. There seemed to be more he wished to say, but before he could speak again, a shower of leaves came spiraling down on top of them. Patience looked up in surprise before hearing the eruption of giggles from behind the tree. Emma and Isabel had found them.

Both twins peeked their heads out from behind the trunk. "Did we startle you?"

Michael laughed. He stooped down to pick up a handful of his own, chasing his sisters to the other side of the trunk.

They shrieked as he threw a showering of leaves just above their heads, letting them fall down over their hair. Patience smiled. She adored the girls as much as Michael seemed to think they adored her, but she did resent them a little in that moment.

Because of their interruption, she hadn't heard what Michael had been about to say. And now she would be far too impatient to discover what it was.

Her heart hammered in her chest. Her patience might have been worth it in one regard. She was fairly certain she had just been granted the indication she had been waiting for. Her forehead still burned from where Michael had touched it, the pressure of his fingertips at her waist still throbbing. Would he have found a reason to touch her, to be so near her, if he viewed her as only a friend?

She didn't allow herself to dwell on the question for long. Only a few months ago, he had viewed her as a monster. *Friend* was much better than that. She would gladly accept it.

A new smile climbed her cheeks as she watched Michael, Emma, and Isabel run through the leaves. Each time Michael laughed or smiled, he glanced back at Patience, sharing the moment with her. Her heart stirred from the slumber she had coaxed it into, becoming more alert with each glance Michael cast her way.

By the time Michael walked toward her, brushing bits of dried leaves from his jacket, her heart was wide awake.

He extended his hand. "Come join us. If you dare."

She took his hand, and he tugged her forward, directly into the fire of Isabel's newest handful of leaves. Patience laughed, throwing her own collection of red leaves at Isabel in retaliation. The game could have gone on forever considering that there was no clear way to choose a winner. Patience hoped that it would. In that moment, she decided that autumn leaves, Isabel and Emma's smiles, and Michael's laugh were three of her favorite things.

She would enjoy them while she could.

CHAPTER EIGHTEEN

*M*ichael's eyes darted to the clock in the corner of his studio. He only had ten minutes to finish his work for the day if he wished to make it back to the drawing room before Patience left. Most days his schedule was filled with clients, but today he had been able to spend several hours on his own projects.

He quickly locked the door to his studio, rushing to clean this brushes and hide the half-length canvas on the easel in front of him. Working from an existing painting was more difficult than working from a live subject, but he had managed to replicate his original painting of Patience quite closely by working from the one he had called *The Monstrous Debutante.* He had promised Patience that he would destroy the piece, but he still needed it for another week or two until he finished the final touches on Patience's new portrait.

He held one brush in his mouth while turning to grab another, adding one detail he had missed before hoisting the canvas off of the easel and propping it against the wall in the far corner. He only had a few minutes to clean if he wished to see Patience before she left.

And he certainly did.

He positioned several rolls of canvas and a few boxes around the new portrait of Patience to conceal it before moving toward his other easel.

The painting of Orpheus and Eurydice was nearly complete, and he was proud of his work. He imagined Father would have been just as proud. Since most of the paint was dry, he had begun hiding the piece in the compartment at the back of his shop, deep within the closet where he stored most of his supplies. Since his fame as an artist had spread, there had been many more people visiting his studio or peering through the windows while he worked. The only two pieces he was protective of were his Orpheus piece, and his new portrait of Patience.

He hid the monstrous portrait with her new portrait, only to ensure it was not seen by anyone passing by the shop. He hoped society would soon forget what she looked like so Patience could venture outside without feeling the need to hide her face.

After locking his studio doors, he began his walk home, scratching at the dried paint on his hands. The very moment his mind was idle, his thoughts traveled to Patience, laughing and spinning in the leaves in her blue pelisse. He had never seen her so happy, and he was fairly certain that the effect it had had on his heart was irreversible. He had been working to pull down the walls that surrounded her for months, and now he was finally seeing the results of his efforts.

What he saw behind those walls was a beauty that matched her exterior. He wanted to know what had caused those walls that had been so difficult to remove. He wanted to know why she still appeared to be clinging to them.

Most of all, he wanted to know what was in her heart, but it seemed to be the most heavily guarded of all.

He found Patience in the drawing room. She was still holding her teacup. Mother, Emma, and Isabel's cups sat on the tea table, completely empty. It might have been in his imagination, but Michael hoped that Patience had intentionally drank hers slower so she might have the opportunity to see him.

It was silly to have such a hope. Dangerous, really. No matter the state of her reputation, he doubted Patience would ever consider him. Just like the rumor she had tried to start at the masquerade, she would reject any proposal he offered her. The history between them was filled with so much tumult. How could her strong feelings of hate ever transform to love? It seemed impossible. But then...hadn't *his* feelings transformed? He banished the thought before he could dwell on it.

Mother stood and gave him a hug as she always did when he returned home each day. Patience sat with her usual stiff posture at the edge of the settee, watching them from over the rim of her teacup. When Mother returned to her place on the sofa, Michael took the empty seat beside Patience on the settee. He cast her a smile in greeting, relieved to see her smile back. He had been worried that the progress he had seen in her the day before had already disappeared. Her eyes lingered on his a little longer than usual before returning to her teacup.

"I have been curious about your painting of Orpheus," Patience said in a quiet voice. "Is it nearly complete?" He caught a hint of color on her cheeks. Had he made her nervous by sitting so close? That was a good sign, wasn't it? He hardly knew. He didn't wish to make her uncomfortable, so he shifted away slightly. Her eyes rose to his again. Was it…disappointment he saw in them?

"Yes." He nodded. "It will be finished within a week or two." He tried to choose his next words carefully. Mother and the twins were distracted with their own conversation, though Michael caught Mother's attention shifting to them on occasion. A sly smile pulled at the corners of her mouth.

He returned his attention to Patience. "Would you like to come see it? I don't have any clients tomorrow between two and three in the afternoon."

She smiled, giving a quick nod of her head. "Yes."

Michael's heart melted, leaving him weak. To know that she admired and cared about his work enough to inquire after it made him like her even more. *Blast it all*, he was not supposed to be dwelling on his feelings. He cleared his throat. "I will see you tomorrow then."

She seemed to take his words as a dismissal, because she made to stand. He grabbed her elbow before she could escape. "Wait." He released his hold on her arm when he caught his sisters watching. Patience sat back down, eyeing him with curiosity. "I was not suggesting that you leave. Please stay for dinner."

Her lips pressed together as she suppressed a look of surprise. No matter how many times he invited her to stay for dinner, she never seemed accustomed to it. Her eyes fluttered up to meet his, shielded partially by her lashes. "Very well."

Did she realize what a puddle she made him? He could hardly breathe as her gaze held him captive. Even with his mother and sisters watching, he might have kissed her, right there on the settee.

Stop. It took all his concentration to keep his gaze away from her lips and the dimple near the corner of her mouth. The last time they had been alone together collecting leaves he had almost told her what she meant to him. He had told her how his family cared for her, but he hadn't managed to tell her how he cared for her. These were different emotions than what his mother and sisters felt for her. The feelings in his chest were to be handled with care and hidden with even more care. It would have been foolish to tell her his feelings when he did not fully understand them himself.

There was much he still didn't know about Patience, and he had a feeling it would require a great deal of patience before he could discover it all.

Patience adjusted her pelisse as the wind caught under her skirts. It was the coldest day of autumn so far. She was grateful for the dropping temperatures. It meant she could wear long sleeves without appearing out of the ordinary. She drew a deep breath before opening the door to Michael's studio. He stood behind his easel, brown hair falling over his forehead, dark brows furrowed in concentration. He balanced a paintbrush in his mouth, holding the other in his right hand as he added strokes to the canvas. His eyes lit up when she entered, and his mouth smiled around the handle of the paintbrush as if he had forgotten he had placed it there.

She laughed at the expression. He removed the paintbrush from his mouth, shaking his head. "You caught me in a very focused state." He wiped his hands on his smock. "Your timing is also most opportune." He flashed her a grin. "Because I just finished my piece of Orpheus and Eurydice."

Patience took one step forward, gasping when she saw the completed piece. The colors were vibrant, the emotions on Orpheus's face palpable. Her heart wrenched as she took in the sorrow and regret in his features as he watched Eurydice slip away. Because of his own mistake, she was lost forever. Patience shook her head in awe. "This is beautiful." She looked up at him. "Truly."

A small smile tugged on his lips. His eyes softened as he met her gaze. "Will you help me give it a name?"

She studied Orpheus, then Eurydice. "Orpheus has more to lose in this moment. I daresay he is the focus of the piece."

"I agree." Michael's eyes flashed with amusement as he observed her analysis.

"Since I refused to allow you to call me Impatience, perhaps that should be what you call this piece. After all, it was Orpheus's impatience which caused him to glance back at Eurydice prematurely, thus causing the gods to keep her in the land of the dead."

Michael's smile grew wider before his expression turned thoughtful. "It was also a lack of trust," he said, rubbing his chin. "He didn't fully believe that she could be transformed."

Patience leaned closer to the canvas, amazed by all the small details that had come together to form this master-piece. Each layer of paint had been carefully placed, every stroke ranging from textured and thick to the width of a single hair. "Do you suppose Eurydice felt abandoned?" The woman's expression was difficult to read in the paint-ing, shadowed as she was. "The man she loved could have saved her, but he failed. I pity Orpheus for his regret, but I pity Eurydice more. She was left there in the darkness alone." Patience's heart stung. She knew how it felt to be abandoned.

Michael was silent for a long moment. "His mistake was great, but their love was greater. I do not doubt that she felt alone, but I'm certain she forgave him."

Patience studied their hands, entwined at the fingertips,

seconds away from being torn apart. "*A Distant Love.* There is a physical distance growing between the two, yet the emotion in their faces shows that the distance will not hinder the love they share. In such a moment of tragedy, there is hope, at least, that their love will live on."

Michael watched her for a long moment, giving a slow nod of approval. "So it shall be called *A Distant Love*. I think it is quite fitting."

"I quite enjoy naming artwork." She walked past Michael, tapping her chin. What else have you painted that still requires a name?" She started toward the back corner of the studio. She only made it a few steps before she heard a paintbrush clatter to the floor. Michael rushed forward, stepping into her path.

She stopped, frowning. His broad shoulders blocked the corner of the room from her view. She rose on her toes, attempting to see over his shoulder. The expression on his face was far too suspicious.

"I have no other paintings in need of names." His smile looked as though *it* had been painted on.

She tipped her head to one side. Why had he rushed in front of her? There was something in that corner that he did not wish for her to see. She tried walking forward again, but he moved with her, anticipating each step that she took in an effort to see around him. "Michael!" She let out a huffed breath.

He gave a nervous laugh. "I think it is time for you to leave. My mother will be expecting you for tea."

"What are you hiding?" She narrowed her eyes at him.

"Nothing."

That was precisely what people said when they were indeed hiding something. She darted around him, but he was too quick. His arms captured her from behind, lifting her completely off of the floor. With her body pressed against Michael's, she could scarcely breathe. She had never felt small before, but by the way he had effortlessly lifted her off her feet, she felt far from masculine—a word Mama had often used in reference to her height. She was only in his arms for a short moment before he rotated her around, setting her back on her feet.

"Go on," he said, just as breathless as she was. "There is nothing more for you to see here." He crossed his arms over his chest—the very chest her back had just been leaning against.

She raised one eyebrow before surrendering with a laugh. Why was he acting so suspicious? She could hardly bear her curiosity. She backed away with slow steps, keeping her narrowed eyes fixed on him so he would have no doubt that she was skeptical.

He followed her until she was outside of his studio. He gave her an apologetic smile before walking back inside and closing the door halfway between them. "Enjoy your tea." His eyes sparked with mischief as he closed the door.

Patience let out a huffed breath. It would bother her all day, yet she was not actually vexed by him. A ridiculous smile had taken root on her face since the moment he had pulled her against him and lifted her off the floor. His arms had fit so perfectly around her. If only she had been allowed more than a few short seconds to feel it. The sensation had already started to fade, much like her better judgement. *Michael is a friend, nothing more. A friend. A friend.* She repeated the words in her mind as she began the short walk to the Cavinders' for tea.

CHAPTER NINETEEN

*P*atience watched the cobblestones as she walked, careful to keep her bonnet low enough to conceal her face. She shivered as a cold wind cut through the sleeves of her pelisse.

Just a few shops away from Michael's studio, she caught sight of a woman sitting alone on the street. Her dirt-streaked dark hair had fallen partially over her eyes, and her arms were wrapped around herself. She shivered, pulling the thin, torn fabric of her shawl around her shoulders. A pang of sympathy struck Patience straight in the heart. The only thing that could have caused this woman to be out in the cold alone would be that she had no where else to go. She didn't even have a way to keep warm.

Patience glanced left and right, noting just a few passersby on that side of the street. Her heart pounded. She knew what she had to do, but the thought terrified her. Before she could lose her nerve, she unbuttoned her pelisse, slipping her arms out of the sleeves. Panic clutched every muscle in her body as she exposed her scars to anyone who looked upon her. Her face was covered, but the puckered skin on her arm was more visible than it had ever been in public.

She hurried toward the woman on the ground. The moment she noticed Patience's approach, she stood, eyes wide.

"Don't be afraid," Patience said, peeking out from under her bonnet. "This is for you." She extended her blue pelisse. The woman's eyes followed Patience's movement.

"Please, ma'am, ye're too generous." She touched the sleeve of the pelisse, shaking her head.

"Take it," Patience instructed. "You must keep yourself warm."

The woman studied Patience from head to toe, shaking her head. "Thank ye, miss." Her face flooded with gratitude as she reached her hands out to gather the pelisse into her arms. She then placed both hands on Patience's shoulders. She held them there for a long time. "Bless ye for yer kind heart." Her hands slipped away, burrowing back under the fabric of the pelisse.

Patience smiled. "You are very welcome. I wish you all the best."

The woman bowed as Patience walked away.

Patience wrapped her arms around herself. She began shivering, walking faster toward the Cavinders' home. Her heart pounded with dread. Now she was left without anything to cover her arms with. Emma and Isabel had already seen her scars, but Mrs. Cavinder had not. What if she was as disgusted by them as Mama was?

Her legs shook as she made her way up the front steps. As soon as she was inside, she would ask to borrow a shawl from Emma or Isabel. She didn't regret giving that woman her pelisse. She had needed it more than Patience had. The woman deserved to be kept warm and—

Patience froze, looking down at her arm. Where was her reticule?

She had draped it over her elbow after taking off the pelisse. She turned around, checking the ground behind her. She would have certainly heard it fall off her elbow. The small bag had been filled with heavy coins, nearly all the money she had brought with her to London. Panic seized her limbs. Where had it gone? She recalled the way the woman on the street had clung to her arms in gratitude, then quickly burrowed her hands back inside the pelisse.

That blasted thief had stolen her reticule.

Anger pulsed in her neck as she paced the front steps, mingling with the anxiety in her chest. The emotion that arose next nearly choked her. Betrayal.

Her heart quickened as she slipped down to the ground, burying her face in her hands as she sat on the steps. Her breath was shallow and fast, her arms and legs shaking. Her stomach twisted, threatening to dispose of its contents. She squeezed her eyes closed, fighting the tears that gathered behind her eyelids. All the pain she had buried the day she had discovered Hattie and Lord

Clitheroe's betrayal was now rising to the surface. She hadn't allowed herself to feel it for months. She had begun to believe and trust in the goodness of people again, but then that woman had stolen her reticule. She gritted her teeth, forcing her emotions back to their proper place. Out of sight. Hidden. Buried.

She took a moment to catch her breath, rising to her feet. She would have taken more time to compose herself, but she wasn't given the chance. The front door opened at the hands of Mrs. Cavinder. The moment her gaze fell on Patience, the smile faded from her lips. "My dear, you must be so cold! Come inside at once."

Patience obeyed, clasping her hands behind her back to hide at least part of her bare arm. Mrs. Cavinder led her to the drawing room, pulling a chair out in front of the hearth. "What were you doing out in this weather without anything to keep warm?" Mrs. Cavinder's gaze barely skimmed over Patience's scars before returning to her face. Not even a hint of surprise or disgust entered her expression, only deep concern.

Patience let out a shaky breath as the fire spread warmth over her skin. "I gave my pelisse to a poor woman on the street. I just realized that she stole my reticule." Her cheeks heated. "In my generosity, she took advantage of me. She acted so grateful, so kind." Patience shook her head. "She had no remorse in her deceit." Just like Hattie. The memories floated closer to the surface again, and her throat tightened.

Mrs. Cavinder shook her head. "That is not fair, is it?"

Patience shook her head, swallowing the lump in her throat. "I should find her and take my pelisse back." She groaned, hiding her face in her hands.

Mrs. Cavinder wrapped one arm around Patience's shoulders. "There is little good that would come from that. It is often the most unkind people who require kindness the most. If this woman truly was poor, she must have needed the money in your reticule desperately. It is no excuse for thievery, mind you, but it is something to consider as you attempt to forgive her."

Patience lifted her face away from her hands. With Mrs. Cavinder's arm wrapped tightly around her shoulders, she felt the threat of tears overwhelm her again. Mrs. Cavinder's eyes were soft and gentle as they looked at her. They were focused on her eyes—her soul—not on the flaws of her skin or the way her tears had likely caused her cheeks to be covered in red splotches. She gave Patience a squeeze, pulling her closer. One hand stroked her hair, guiding Patience's head to her shoulder.

Patience closed her eyes as a tear slipped down the bridge of her nose. She couldn't recall the last time—if ever—that she had been held like this. Comforted and understood. Growing up at Briarwood, she had been *bred, reared, educated*—but she had never been *mothered* or *nurtured*. Had she even been loved? She bit her lip to keep from sobbing into Mrs. Cavinder's shoulder, because during those years of being bred, she had been advised to keep her emotions from showing.

She swallowed hard, thinking of Mrs. Cavinder's words.

Forgiveness was not as simple as it seemed. It was far easier to forgive someone who showed regret and pain over their actions. Patience hadn't taken long to forgive Mr. Cavinder because of this. Perhaps that again showed the superiority of his character, because he had forgiven her *before* she had shown any remorse. She hadn't deserved his kindness, but he had given it freely, just as Mrs. Cavinder did now.

Patience, as an unkind person, had needed kindness the most.

Her heart softened a little toward the woman in town. Patience had been just like her only a few months before. Intent only to take, not to give. When so much had been taken from her, Patience had become bitter and cruel, clinging to what little she had.

Her heart stung again as she thought of Hattie's betrayal. Was that also something she was expected to forgive? The idea tortured Patience's heart, and her entire body refused the idea. The bitterness and anger she felt were the only things that protected her from the pain. If those feelings were gone, she would be left raw and vulnerable, and then what would she do?

Mrs. Cavinder held her close for several minutes, stroking her hair. The turmoil in her chest had just begun to calm when the drawing room door opened again. The sound startled her. She sat upright, turning away from the hearth to see who had entered the room.

It was Michael.

Her hands shook as she looked down, remembering that her arms were uncovered. Shame heated her cheeks, and she felt a sudden, wild desperation to cover herself, to hide from his view. It had been more than a year since he had seen her scars, so she had hoped he had forgotten just how unsightly they were. She whirled back toward the hearth, heart thudding past her ears.

"I finished early today," he said, a smile in his voice.

Michael's footfalls were barely audible past her pulse as he walked into the room and sat in the chair adjacent to hers. She refused to look at him, though she felt his gaze burning against her skin. The room faded into silence, and Patience couldn't bear to be there a moment longer.

"Excuse me," she said in a choked whisper. Rising to her feet, she rushed from the room, passing Michael without looking at him. She didn't dare look at his face for the risk of seeing disgust written upon it. The hall was cool, and it served as a balm to the shame on her cheeks. As quickly as she could, she started toward the front door. She had only made it halfway when she heard heavy footfalls coming up behind her.

"Patience—" Michael's voice stopped her in her tracks. "Where are you going?"

She clasped her hands in front of her, pulling her arms away from his view. Where *was* she going? It was cold outside, and she didn't want to walk in public without long sleeves again. She hadn't been thinking as she fled from the drawing room. All she had wanted was to avoid Michael while she was so vulnerable. "I don't know." She stared at the door handle, just a few paces in front of her. If she dashed forward, she could escape. But her feet kept her rooted to the floor.

Michael stepped around her until he faced her completely. Her breath hitched, her legs shaking all over again. Her anxiety and emotions had already been fragile that day, but with Michael standing in front of her, eyes kind and free of judgment like his mother's, her composure wavered.

He searched her face. The warmth in his eyes unraveled her, thread by thread. "Patience." He shook his head. His eyes lowered to her scars, concern knitting his brow. Ever so slowly, his fingers lifted to the puckered skin on her right arm, tracing over it. Her heart pounded. How could he bear to touch them? It wasn't disgust in his expression. It was sorrow.

"How did this happen? What hurt you?" His voice was hoarse. "You can trust me."

A tear slipped from her eye, then another. She licked her lips, trying to pull the lump in her throat back to its proper place, but her tears fell freely. She sniffed, shaking her head. "It doesn't matter."

"Yes, it does." Michael's eyes flashed with frustration. His hands slid to her shoulders, gripping softly to keep her stable. "Anything that hurts you, anything you feel matters to *me*." The sincerity of his words brought another sob out of her.

Her posture slumped, her chin dropping to her chest. She had never told anyone the truth about that day. Not even Mama. Not Papa. Hattie had begged her not to, and she had listened. "Ten years ago, my parents left my older sister Hattie and me alone for a day. As my older sister, Hattie was given authority to care for me while they were away." Patience rubbed at her nose, staring at the buttons on Michael's waistcoat and the streaks of dried paint on his wrists. "W-we went to the kitchen while our cook was gathering herbs in the garden. Hattie wished to steal a tray of cakes while the cook was not aware. I had always feared disappointing my parents and acting against their instruction, so I did not support Hattie's mischief." Patience swallowed, her words spilling out faster. "We began arguing, and we both became angry. Hattie tried to reach for the cakes, but I stopped her. She was furious that I would not listen to her. When she pushed me aside, I pushed her back. We had argued often, but we had never hurt one another." Patience wiped at the fresh tears on her cheeks. "I never thought Hattie would hurt me, but that day she was more angry than I had ever seen her. We were both children, so she likely didn't fully realize what the consequences of her actions would be." Patience fell silent, the secret lodged in her throat.

"What did she do?" His voice was filled with apprehension.

Patience took a deep breath. "She lifted the pot of boiling water from behind me and poured it over my arm." Her jaw tightened. "When she realized what she had done, she begged me not to tell our parents. I didn't wish to cause trouble, so I told them the story Hattie invented. In her story, I was playing in the kitchen and accidentally knocked over the pot. To this day, that is what they believe. Hattie is an angel in their eyes, unable to do wrong. It took me many years to fully recognize her true nature, no matter how often she hurt me."

"She has hurt you more than once?" Michael wiped at the tears on her cheeks, holding her face between his hands. His brow was furrowed with concern and anger, as if he wished to confront Hattie himself. She had no choice but to look at him, and it broke her composure in two. A sob shook her body as she nodded.

"The worst of it happened just before I came to London. Lord Clitheroe is just as much to blame, but my sister's betrayal hurt far more than his." She squeezed her eyes closed as tears slid down her face toward Michael's fingers. "I always suspected that there was something between them. Lord Clitheroe was not secretive about his opinion of Hattie's beauty, and she never failed to flirt with any man, eligible or not. I thought once she was married her habits would change, but I was wrong." She choked on a sob. "One week before my wedding, I saw her kiss him." All the emotions she had been suppressing came pouring out, all the secrets she had been holding in her heart were now on full display. Michael wiped away more of her tears before pulling her against his chest. His arms wrapped around her, tight and secure.

"I was still willing to marry him, even after what I had seen. It was the only way my parents would have loved me." Her voice cracked. "I have always wondered if they would have loved me more if my arm had not been burned.

If-if there hadn't been a part of me my mother was always seeking to hide."

"That is not love," Michael said, his voice close to her ear. "If their love for you has such conditions, then it is not worth seeking. There are others who will love you the way you deserve to be loved."

She buried her face in his chest, letting his shirt soak up what remained of her tears. She breathed deeply, the smell of him serving to relax her senses. Others? Was Michael one of these others? A surge of longing washed over her heart. He rested his chin on top of her head, rubbing reassuring circles over the space between her shoulder blades. Fresh tears spilled from her eyes as he held her. She already knew he wouldn't let go. He would keep his arms wrapped around her until she pulled away. He would be there no matter how long she needed him. She had never felt more secure, warm, or safe.

Michael's voice came again, slow and deliberate. "I want you to forget everything you have been taught by your mother and remember this one lesson. People are not paintings."

Patience listened, wrapping her arms around the back of his jacket, clinging to the fabric there with as much fastness as she clung to each of his words. "What do you mean?"

"The value of a painting is determined by its appearance. They are created to be looked at. People are not paintings," he repeated. "We are created to love and to be loved, to learn, grow, be happy, and experience life. What is the value of that life if it is lived without that understanding? Please, do not forget how inherently valuable you are. Never allow anyone to convince you otherwise."

Patience sniffed, lifting her head from Michael's chest. She stared up at him, suddenly embarrassed to have been clinging so tightly to his jacket. "You have come far from the man who depicted me as a vile creature." She hadn't felt so shy around him in a very long time. She had just poured her heart out to him, and he had listened.

He framed her shoulders with his hands, rubbing her upper arms softly as he laughed. His eyes settled on hers. "Well, you have come far from the woman who inspired me to create that piece." He paused, a crease forming in his brow. "And now I see who the true monster has always been. I am sorry your sister has been so cruel." His voice was edged in frustration.

Patience thought of Mrs. Cavinder's words of advice about forgiving the woman who had stolen her reticule. Would forgiving Hattie be enough to lift the weight that had been bearing down on her back? If she thought she were capable of forgiving her sister, then she would try, but each time she thought of her, all she felt was bitterness and pain. "Do you think I need to forgive her?" Patience asked, her voice weak.

Michael studied her face, a hint of disbelief in his features. "If you are willing to try, I think that is already more than most people could manage."

Patience's head ached from all her crying. She closed her eyes. "I'm not certain it is possible."

His fingers brushed a strand of wet hair from her cheek, sending tendrils of warmth over her skin. "It will not happen instantly. It will take time, and that is nothing to be ashamed of."

Patience nodded, opening her eyes. "Thank you, Michael." Her lip quivered as she was overcome with emotion again. She had turned into a watering pot. "You..." her voice faded. What had she meant to say? There were a thousand compliments that she could have given him, so many words she could have used to convey what he meant to her without being too forward, but she couldn't grasp onto a single one.

He raised his eyebrows as he waited for her to finish her blank sentence.

"You are..." She pressed her lips together, sniffing. "You are my favorite..." Her brow scrunched as she searched for the right word. He was her favorite *what* exactly? Friend? Artist? Cavinder? Member of the human race? "You are my favorite." A frustrated breath escaped her as a smile tugged on his lips. He was amused with her awkwardness once again. Before she could make a fool of herself further, she slipped away from his arms. Walking back to the drawing room, she felt his gaze on her back. She was glad he did not follow her. She needed to borrow a shawl from Mrs. Cavinder and be on her way.

When she opened the door, she found Mrs. Cavinder sitting in the same chair she had been sitting in when Patience left the room. Before she could even ask, Mrs. Cavinder pulled the shawl away from her own shoulders, standing to wrap it around Patience. "I have called for a carriage to take you home. It is far too cold for you to walk."

The simple kindness of the gesture flooded her heart with gratitude. The two words that formed her reply would never be enough, but still, she spoke them again.

"Thank you."

CHAPTER TWENTY

*R*ubbing his palms on his breeches did little to calm Michael's nerves. He had taken two days to prepare himself, yet he was still a complete disaster. He had invented dozens of excuses, reasons to be a coward rather than face his fear of inviting Patience to go on a ride with him.

The weather could be too cold.

Patience could wish to stay indoors rather than venture out in public.

She could be embarrassed to be near him after their last interaction.

And then who would be their chaperone? His mother? The idea did not sit comfortably with his stomach. His heart thudded in his chest as he paced in front of the front steps of his townhouse.

He had left his studio later than usual. At any moment,

Patience would step out the front doors to leave tea and catch him in his distress.

He removed his hat, raking a hand over his hair as he let out a long exhale. What the devil was he doing? He could not pursue the daughter of an earl—the worst earl of his acquaintance, no less. His fame had elevated his pride too much. It had blinded him to the reality of his station. But since Patience had opened her heart to him, trusting him enough to take down her walls, his feelings for her had only grown. He wanted to plant a facer on Lord Clitheroe and send her sister on a boat across the world where she would never hurt Patience again. He would have a few select words for her parents as well. It only made sense that Lord Ryecombe would have chosen a wife, Patience's mother, who was just as vile as he was.

Each second that Michael was not with Patience was its own agony, and he found that his thoughts could settle on nothing but her. Her smile, her voice, each laugh that took all his effort to win; it was all engraved on his heart like the markings on his mother's necklace, unique and familiar. It was as if his heart had been trained to love Patience from the day he was created.

Gads, man, he scolded himself. He was too much of a romantic for his own good.

The front door opened behind him. He whirled around, clutching his hat in front of him. Patience stood in the doorway, hazel eyes round with surprise. Ivory fabric draped the long, curved lines of her figure, and dark ringlets framed her cheeks beneath her bonnet. "Did I give you a fright?" she asked, a smile tilting her lips.

Michael dipped his head with a laugh. "Perhaps a little." He walked up two steps until he stood on the one just below her. "Are you leaving?"

She stared at him, biting her lower lip nervously. "Well, I—" she paused, searching his face.

He continued to stand there like a ninny until he remembered that this was usually the moment he invited her to dinner. She seemed to be expecting that invitation, hoping for it even. That gave him the confidence he needed to find his elusive words. "There are two invitations I would like to extend to you," he said.

Her eyebrows lifted. "Two?"

"Yes." Michael took a deep breath. "The first may be obvious. By now you should know never to plan to leave without staying for dinner."

She looked down at the ground as she laughed.

"The second one…" he swallowed, shifting on his feet. Even though he had spent hours planning, he still couldn't find the correct words. Rather than follow his original plan, a new one sprang to mind. "I am taking my sisters to Covent Garden Theatre next week for a ballet. I thought you might like to accompany us." This plan would be more comfortable for Patience, yet it would still give him the opportunity to spend more time with her.

Her features grew serious. "Is it wise for me to venture to such a public place? I'm afraid the exhibition was still too recent. And if I am recognized there…with you…"

"Then we shall give society something new to talk about." Michael tipped his head to one side with a smile. "You cannot hide forever."

"I am quite comfortable hiding, actually." She gave a weak grin.

"Please, come. My sisters will miss you if you don't." He cleared his throat. "As will I."

She met his gaze, careful and slow. "I will come, but only if you promise to shield me from any gossipmongers."

"I will consider it my duty." Michael gave a deep bow, earning another laugh from her. He glanced up, his head still lowered. "Do you accept my services, then?"

"Yes." The width of her smile set his worries at ease. Their friendship had become too dear to him to risk ruining it. This was not a formal courtship. They were simply taking his sisters to the theatre.

He had never liked crowded social events. Yet he could hardly wait to attend.

<hr />

They were seated in the back row of the balcony, elevated above row after row of elegant men and women. From Michael's vantage point, he could clearly observe just why he found events like this so repulsive. Many of these people hadn't come to see the ballet, but to *be seen* by everyone else. The excessive expense that was placed on hair arrangements, gowns, and the foppish accessories of the upper class men made Michael's stomach turn. He had witnessed the same things at the Royal Academy's exhibition. The theatre was lit with hundreds of candles, trimmed in gold and velvet all around. The stage was set and prepared for the production.

Emma and Isabel observed the crowd, whispering to one another in a much more polite manner than they would have before, sitting with perfect posture in their velvet seats, polite smiles on their lips. Patience had taught them well. She sat just as properly, with her spine straight and hands folded in her lap beside him. Her face, however, lacked the polite smile. Her brow was knit together with nervousness as her gaze darted to the rows of people surrounding them.

Michael leaned close to her ear, enjoying the scent of roses she carried. "If it comes to it, I will remove my jacket and drape it over your head, then carry you up the stairs and out those doors." He gestured behind them.

Patience cast him a skeptical look, the corners of her mouth quivering upward. "I think that would cause a much more embarrassing spectacle."

He gave a quiet laugh, and she joined him. He eyed her gloved hand, now sitting on the armrest beside him. How untoward would it be if he held it? He fought the urge to entwine his fingers with hers. He could already imagine her wriggling her hand away from his grip and scolding him for his public affection. If there were a way to make it not public, then he might have tried. He didn't know how long Patience would be in London, and he had begun to sense that he was running out of time.

His chances of winning her heart might have been slim, but he would loathe himself forever if he didn't at least try.

He refused to experience the torturous regret that Orpheus felt when he lost Eurydice due to his own mistake.

The production began, and the light in their section of the balcony was dimmed. The scent of smoke filled the air as the candles on the walls around them went out and the stage was brightened. The crowd released a collective sigh, whispers of delight undulating through the audience.

"This is much better," Patience whispered in his ear. His heart stalled as her breath rustled his collar. "If I wish to remain hidden, darkness shall be my ally." She gave a quiet laugh, returning her gaze to the stage below.

He laughed, but it sounded forced. He could hardly focus on anything but his own nervousness—and foolishness—as he glanced down at her hand. Michael's pulse pounded. Before his fortitude could slip away, he placed his elbow on the armrest, directly beside hers.

Their forearms touched. She didn't pull away.

He was aware of every single one of her movements, even the moment when her breathing was interrupted. It was the same moment he gathered the nerve to wrap his fingers around hers. He traced his thumb in a circle over the top of her wrist, trailing the caress down to her hand before entwining his fingers in hers. A flame flickered in his chest when her eyes found his in the dark.

He leaned toward her ear. "I'll stop if you wish. I know

you don't wish for any rumors to be spread." He awaited her reply, holding his breath.

"N-no. I believe it is dim enough, and people are distracted by the production..." her voice trailed off. Michael smiled to himself. He had made her flustered.

"It seems the darkness is my ally as well," he whispered.

He wished he could have seen Patience's expression at his flirting. What sort of ally was the darkness if it prevented him from seeing the color he might have brought to her cheeks? He continued tracing shapes over the back of her hand, creating strokes like he did on his paintings.

He was glad Emma and Isabel were enjoying the production. He was fairly certain that by the end of it, he wouldn't remember a single thing. And if his efforts to woo her were successful, Patience wouldn't either.

When the curtains were closed and the candles lit, Michael finally slipped his hand away. As light returned to the room, he stole a glance at Patience's face. The smile she gave him was shy and endearing, and it brought a smile to his own face that was likely far too wide to be inconspicuous. His heart hammered in his chest. He never would have thought holding a woman's hand through a pair of gloves could be so thrilling. But then, perhaps that was only because he had never been in love before.

The danger of the situation caught up to him, nipping at his heels like an angry hound. Patience was unpredictable. She had been through much heartache, and he couldn't place his hopes in any future with her. Even if she did have feelings for him, she could be gone in an instant, choosing the path she had been raised to pursue over a path with him. How could he trust that she had completely changed? Just a few months before, she had come to London with one purpose: to seek revenge on him. Was he a fool to believe that now she cared for him as deeply as he cared for her?

No matter how many worries spiraled through his mind, his heart ignored them, batting them away like cricket balls. As they walked back to their waiting coach, Michael sat on the seat beside Patience, not daring to risk holding her hand again with his sisters facing them on the opposite side of the cramped conveyance. While Emma and Isabel prattled on and on about their favorite things about the theatre, Michael sat comfortably listening, simply happy to see his sisters so happy—and to have Patience beside him.

"Did you enjoy the production?" he asked.

Patience nodded, just as shy as she had been before. "Yes."

"What was your favorite moment of the ballet?"

She was silent for several seconds, and he could practically see her mind at work. He suppressed his smile. Perhaps he had distracted her as much as he had hoped.

"I enjoyed all of it." She paused. "What was your favorite part?" Her voice was filled with curiosity. The carriage passed over a bump in the road, causing Patience to jostle closer to him. Her leg pressed against his, and he found that his own mind had gone blank.

"I enjoyed the whole of it as well." His gaze roamed her face, falling to her lips. Perhaps he could fulfill his original plan of removing his jacket and draping it over Patience's head. Then he might not be so tempted to kiss her.

He barely caught sight of her minuscule smile as she turned toward the window. He didn't know what exactly his actions that night had meant to her, but he knew that something had changed. He sensed it in the way she looked at him. After the carriage had jostled her closer, she hadn't moved away.

Defining his next step would be more difficult. He would have to tread carefully. A proposal would be too sudden, and the thought of declaring his feelings was too intimidating. He needed to know without a doubt that his feelings were reciprocated before he dared do such a thing.

If he could not tell her, then he would have to show her.

CHAPTER TWENTY-ONE

*T*he leaves on the trees grew more colorful by the day, still clinging to the final months of life. October was Patience's favorite month, even if the weather was growing colder. After giving away her blue pelisse, she had planned to purchase a new one. Since her reticule had been stolen, however, she hadn't had enough money to afford it. Thankfully not all her money had been inside the reticule, but the funds that did remain in her room at Mary's house were growing slim.

Patience hadn't meant to eavesdrop, but she had heard Mary and her husband speaking in the breakfast room one morning.

"How long do you suppose she plans to stay?" Mary's husband John had asked in a quiet voice.

Mary's reply had taken several seconds to come. "I didn't think it would be this long."

"Nor did I."

"Well, we cannot turn her away. You know how the Hansfords have practically banished her. My conscience will not allow it."

An exasperated sigh had come from John. "She cannot stay here forever."

"I suppose you are right. Shall we try to find her a husband?"

"With her reputation? I daresay that is unlikely."

"Well, what do you suppose we do?"

"Write to the Hansfords. See if they will allow her to come home. Nearly six months have passed since the exhibition. Perhaps their shame has been forgotten."

The clattering of dishes had indicated that Mary was leaving the table. Patience had hurried down the hall and out of sight.

Dread had puddled in her stomach, giving rise to the uncertainty she had been trying to avoid. Mary and John had been generous in taking her in, but she now saw how it burdened them. She had once been hoping for and awaiting a letter from her parents, but she no longer expected one to come. Mary and John were right—she could not stay with them forever. Was marriage truly her only hope? She had other relatives who might take her in, but none who lived in London.

And it broke her heart to think that she might not always live so close to the Cavinders. To Michael.

The days passed far too quickly. Already three had passed since he had held her hand at the theatre. She had been so hopeful then, but now she was back in the depths of worry, wondering if she had imagined the entire thing. He seemed to have carried on as though nothing romantic had happened between them. He was cautious around her, more than he ever had been. Did he require more encouragement? The last time Patience had tried to encourage a man into matrimony had resulted in a disaster. She was too afraid to lose Michael and the friendship they shared. She had never treasured something so much.

If he did have feelings for her, which she suspected that he did, then what was he waiting for? If only he knew how readily she would accept any proposal he offered her, and not simply because she relied on marriage to secure her future.

She loved him.

Admitting it to herself had been terrifying, but she had finally accepted the truth. As Michael had said, *people are not paintings. They are created to love and to be loved, to learn, grow, be happy, and experience life.* What value would her life have if Michael was not in it? Without him, she would live out her years as empty and lifeless as a painting, just as she had lived the first twenty-one years of her life. The thought of going back to the loneliness of her past sent panic spiraling through her core.

She stared out the window of her bedchamber on the second floor of Mary and John's townhouse. From her vantage point, she could see the street of Michael's studio. She had dined with his family the night before, yet she already missed him. His flirtations had been subtle since the theatre, disguised in the amused smiles they shared across the table as Emma and Isabel swooned over the gentlemen they had seen at one event or another. They hadn't been alone together for longer than a few seconds at a time, so she couldn't have expected him to declare his feelings for her.

She had tried to triumph over her greatest fault, but her efforts were futile.

She had never been so impatient in her entire life.

What could she do to encourage him? She thought of the day she had 'practiced' her flirting with Michael in order to ensure she would be prepared to flirt with Lord Clitheroe. She never would have imagined that one day she would be planning a way to flirt with Michael in earnest.

She had never visited his shop uninvited, but at the moment, it was the best option she could think of. If she paid him an unexpected visit, he might begin to realize that she missed him while they were apart. Her heart pounded with sudden nervousness. What if he was busy with a client and turned her away? The excuses could have multiplied all afternoon. She needed to go before she could be persuaded by them.

Excitement guided her movements as she wrapped her cloak around her shoulders, tying her bonnet ribbons and starting out the door. When she reached the outside of Michael's studio, she froze.

A group of women walked down the street, pointing up at the wooden sign above his studio. The pairing of matrons leading the pack prickled in Patience's mind with familiarity.

Could they be the women from the masquerade months before?

They had been wearing masks then, but their stature and air was what made them recognizable. The rumors Patience had started about Michael had thankfully never made it to the papers, but by the way the two older women glared at the doors of Michael's shop, she could only assume that they still believed her.

The woman leading the group squinted, catching sight of Patience from across the street. Given her unique height, Patience was likely just as recognizable as the other women were to her. With their affinity for gossip, they were likely quite curious as to why Patience, who had acted so afraid of Michael, would be entering his studio.

"Drat," she muttered to herself. She quickly slipped through the doors, glancing around the room for Michael. He looked up from his easel, eyes round with surprise. In an instant, he set down his brush, his expression melting into a smile. "Patience?" He turned the easel toward the corner, stepping out from behind it. He quickly tossed a sheet over the other easel nearby before stuffing his hands into the front pockets of his smock. She recalled his suspicious behavior the last time she had been in his studio when she had tried to see what he had been hiding in the corner of the room.

He strode toward her with a smile, distracting her from her suspicion. His hair had fallen over his brow, his shirt-sleeves rolled in their usual way. His brown eyes appeared lighter when he faced the front window, and the spattering of freckles on his cheeks made Patience's heart skip.

She nearly forgot about the pack of women approaching from outside.

"What has brought you here?" Michael asked. "Is something amiss?" He followed her gaze out the window, a furrow in his brow.

"The women from the masquerade," she whispered, true panic climbing her spine. Why did she feel as though they were being pursued by a real pack of predators? "They have come for you."

Michael's eyes widened. "What, pray tell, does that mean?"

She laughed, letting out a small shriek as she caught sight of the women as they crossed the street behind a passing carriage. Her gaze darted around the room, settling on the open closet in the back corner.

"We must hide." Without thinking, she clutched his wrist, pulling him along as she raced toward the closet. Michael's laugh rustled her hair as she tugged him into the closet, surprised by her own strength. Just seconds before the chime sounded on the front door, Patience tugged the closet door closed, sealing them inside.

The space was much smaller than Patience had expected. Shelves lined each side, leaving only a narrow walkway toward the back of the closet, just a few paces long. Very little light managed to seep into the enclosed space, but Patience's eyes had adjusted enough to see Michael's outline.

"You nearly made me step on my painting of Orpheus," he said, chuckling. She glanced back as he slipped the painting into a hidden compartment at the back of the closet. "This is the only place it will be safe. I keep it here every night." He covered the opening with a sheet from the nearby shelf. His movements were far too loud.

She held a finger to her lips, instructing him to be quiet as she listened to the sounds beyond the doorway. Michael's shoulders shook with suppressed laughter, making her own difficult to keep at bay.

"Mr. Cavinder?" A voice called from the front of the studio. Several feet moved over the creaking floorboards.

"Where is he?"

"How unprofessional that he is not even present at his own studio during the day."

"Did we expect any better from him?"

"No, indeed."

Patience was grateful that Michael was laughing, otherwise she would have felt guilty for inspiring the women to develop such a strong dislike for him.

"But where is the woman who walked in before us? I am certain I saw her enter through the front doors."

Patience held her breath.

"You must be mistaken. There is no one here." The creaking, clicking footfalls resumed. "Come, we have many errands to attend to."

Patience listened carefully as the door chimed again, not daring to move until several seconds had passed after the last footfall sounded. When she was certain all the women were gone, a laugh burst out of her chest. Her stomach ached as she turned to face Michael, who laughed just as heartily.

She tried to shift back a step, but there was no room in the closet amid the boxes that had been placed on the floor between the shelves. She was trapped, pinned between the door and Michael. Her eyes had adjusted more now, enough that she could see the finer details of his face.

His smiling lips, in particular, caught her attention.

Michael's laughter subsided. He seemed to recognize the impropriety of their situation the same moment she did. Her heart gave a thud when his gaze flickered to her mouth.

"It seems we have narrowly escaped with our lives," he said, his voice quiet.

"Indeed." Patience tried to smile, but she lacked the energy it required. She couldn't think of anything witty to say, not when Michael was standing so close. His gaze lifted to hers for a short moment before flickering back to her lips again. Her heart was on fire. This was the opportunity she had been waiting for, wasn't it? Her pulse pounded in her neck. She hadn't anticipated being alone in a closet with Michael, but that was where her trip to his studio had brought her.

Frustration built in her chest as the seconds ticked by. Was he too noble to fill the mere inches that separated his mouth from hers? The restraint in his eyes was obvious, staring back at her like a reflection of her own heart. She wanted to feel his arms around her again, taste his lips, surrender to the pull she felt toward him.

And she was through with being patient.

She drew a breath as she pulled his head down to hers. In immediate, or perhaps simultaneous response, his hands seized her by the waist, his mouth meeting hers halfway in the space between them. Her heart was on fire. His lips parted hers, soft and gentle at first, gradually growing in intensity. But she did not want his gentle, cautious kisses, not after she had waited so long. She gripped the front of his smock in two handfuls of fabric, and suddenly he was kissing her deeper, harder, his hands racing over her back and arms and eventually settling on the sides of her face.

He kissed her with a fervent urgency that she had never felt before, backing her against the closet door. Every nerve in her body tremored with emotion. She inhaled the clean soap on his skin and the scent that reminded her of a fresh roll of canvas or the pages of a new book. Even with him pressing her against the door, kissing her mouth as though his life depended on it, she still needed him closer. She needed him to never, ever stop.

She caressed the sides of his jaw, burying her fingers in his soft hair. A low groan sounded in the back of his throat. She didn't care that it was a dark and dust-covered closet where Michael kissed her. She didn't care one bit. The only thing her senses could detect was him. *Michael Cavinder*. His mouth on hers, his taste, his scent, his hands against her face.

"Patience," he whispered against her lips. He pulled

away with another groan. Their foreheads still touched, even the bridges of their noses. It was cruel of him to stop kissing her if he was going to keep his lips so close to hers.

Her eyelids fluttered open, heavy and weak. She traced her fingers over the buttons of his waistcoat, watching the quick rise and fall of his chest.

"Perhaps we should leave," he traced his thumb over her cheek, his eyes wary. A smile tugged his mouth upward, and it took all her energy not to kiss his grinning lips again. How long had they been in that closet? Time had paused just for them. Patience's heart felt as though it had been turned upside down and shaken before being pressed back into her chest. Opposite, but still the same, experiencing love in a way it never had before.

She didn't want to leave. Uncertainty and sorrow didn't live inside that closet. It was Patience and Michael, Orpheus and Eurydice, and a few painting supplies.

Despite how her entire being protested, she knew Michael was right. If she stayed there much longer, they would surely kiss again, and this time they might not have been able to stop. The cramped space thrummed with unspoken feelings. Patience had been kissed by Lord Clitheroe and it had been nothing in comparison to what she had just experienced with Michael. She could only conclude that he cared for her just as much as she hoped. Perhaps even more.

He reached behind her, tugging on the door handle. The door jostled in the frame, but it didn't open. Patience shuffled against the door until she was out of his way. He pulled on the handle again, pushing his shoulder against the door. It didn't budge.

"Is it…stuck?" Patience helped him push.

"I'm afraid so." His eyes met hers. "I have never closed the door behind me before. It has always been a bit difficult, but it has never stuck this firmly before." He shook the handle, thrusting his shoulder against the center of the door again.

"Are we—are we trapped?" She was not being helpful with all her questions.

He turned to face her, laughing as he raked a hand over his hair.

"Leaving is not an option then," Patience said.

"No."

She could think of one way they could pass the time, but she didn't think it wise to tempt him with the suggestion. Her heart was still on fire from their last kiss. She stepped forward, shaking the door handle again. She kicked the base of the door. The resulting click was encouraging. Michael kicked the base of the door even harder while Patience turned the handle. It swung open.

In the commotion, they must have failed to hear the chime of the front entrance. An elderly man stood near Michael's desk, jaw dropping as he took in the scene. Patience stumbled out of the closet, squinting against the brightness of the studio with its many windows. Her lips still tingled, her legs still shaking beneath her. Could the man see that she had just been thoroughly kissed? She glanced back at Michael, who seemed to have just noticed the man.

"Did you know that closet has a secret compartment?" Patience blurted to the man, hoping to somehow explain what they had been doing in the closet together without *truly* explaining what they had been doing. She laughed, a shaky sound. She was still recovering, and likely would be, for a very long time. "Mr. Cavinder stored my portrait there and when I followed him inside to see it, the door stuck behind us."

The man scratched at his long side whiskers, giving a half-hearted nod. He didn't seem to completely believe her, but it was enough to keep his suspicions at bay. She continued her act, offering a bow to Michael as she turned her back to the gentleman with the long side whiskers. Michael's eyes danced with amusement as she lifted her voice to speak again. "I thank you for your time, Mr. Cavinder."

He offered a bow in return before striding toward the man at his desk. "Thank you, Lady Patience." He glanced back at her, casting her flirtatious smile meant just for her.

Legs still shaking, she made her way toward the front door. She only made it a few steps before a fresh grin pulled across her face. She was fairly certain she had never been so happy. Michael hadn't spoken his feelings aloud, but he had given her every indication that he did not view her as a mere *friend.*

The thought made a lump form in her throat. Tears sprung to her eyes as her smile stretched even wider.

He might have even had it in his mind to marry her.

Michael greeted the man at his desk, apologizing for the delay. Patience sneaked around them, her gaze catching on the two easels Michael had been standing behind when she had first arrived. The sheet had slipped off the corner of the one closest to her.

Her stomach plummeted. She could only see half of it, but it was the only half she needed to see to recognize the piece. It was *The Monstrous Debutante*. She frowned. Hadn't Michael promised to destroy it? Why did he still have it in his shop? Not only that, but it was on an easel, as if he were working on it again.

She fought the unease that spread in her veins as she continued walking, tearing her gaze away from the portrait before Michael could realize what she had seen. It must have been what he had been hiding in the corner of his studio the last time she had been there.

He had been acting so suspicious, and now she understood why.

A hint of betrayal climbed over her skin, but she shook it away. There could have been a very reasonable explanation that she was missing.

The concept of optimism was fragile and new, like a butterfly fresh from its cocoon. She tried to cling to it, but her doubts threatened to tear it down. There was a simple solution. All she had to do was ask him, and she would do just that the next day. After all that had passed between them that afternoon, she didn't think it wise to go straight to his house for tea with his mother and sisters. She needed a little time alone to clear her head.

Without looking back, she walked out of the studio and into the autumn air, fighting the sudden sting in her heart and the question that plagued her mind.

What if Michael's opinion of her was not as high as she hoped?

CHAPTER TWENTY-TWO

*A*rising at dawn was much easier when Michael had something to look forward to, even if he had spent half the night awake. His thoughts had been swallowed by Patience and how they had kissed in the closet and how ridiculously happy that fact made him. He hadn't stopped smiling since she had stumbled out of the closet and explained the incident to the customer at his desk. Perhaps he should have been concerned with her ability to lie so convincingly, but he had only been grateful that she had saved him from the man's scrutiny.

He dressed quickly before heading out the door toward his studio. The sun was still in the process of rising. He had a busy schedule that day, so he needed to arrive at his studio early enough to finish his new portrait of Patience before his scheduled appointments. He had been so close to finishing the day before—until Patience had arrived and thoroughly distracted him.

He couldn't quite recall how it had started, but he was fairly certain that she had initiated their kiss. He could no longer doubt that she returned his feelings, so he had begun planning when and how he might propose. He hadn't told his mother or his sisters of his plans yet, though they had questioned many times why he had appeared so jovial the day before. He didn't blame Patience for not joining them for tea that day. She would have likely been questioned as thoroughly as he had been.

Until an engagement was official between them, it was better that she keep her distance.

He approached his studio, squinting against the sunlight that reflected off the glass.

The *broken* glass.

His stomach plummeted. He rushed forward, crushing fragments of glass underfoot as he walked to the front door. The window beside it had been shattered. His heart pounded in his throat as he forced his key into the lock, entering the studio. At first glance, everything appeared to still be where he had left it the day before. But then he noticed the closet.

The door was halfway open. Dread climbed his spine as he ran across the room. He immediately walked to the back of the closet, and his worst fear was confirmed. The small compartment where he had hidden his new painting for the exhibition was open and empty.

Someone had stolen his painting of Orpheus and Eurydice—the project he had spent months completing.

He interlocked his fingers on top of his head, taking

several deep breaths as he paced the length of the closet. He checked every other hiding place he had established in his studio until hopelessness engulfed him.

It was gone.

He searched the corner where he had placed his new portrait of Patience to dry. It was still there, along with *The Monstrous Debutante*. The thief must not have seen it, otherwise he surely would have stolen the famous painting instead of the one Michael hadn't even submitted to the exhibition yet. He tipped his head back with a groan. He should have been more careful. He had often left the Orpheus painting uncovered while clients were present. Any of them could have seen the potential in the piece and planned to steal it, as well as any number of people from outside in the street.

A thought made his skin go cold. But how could they have known where he hid it? He hadn't told anyone where he kept the painting in the compartment at the back of his closet.

He hadn't told anyone except Patience.

He scowled down at the fragments of glass that had spilled into the inside of his studio. A suspicion entered the dark, dusty corners of his mind, but he shoved it away with both hands.

No.

He knew Patience. He knew she would never do something like that, not anymore at least. That thought made him pause.

Not *anymore*.

There had been a time, not very long ago, that she had been capable of worse things than she seemed to be capable of now. His chest tightened as doubt continued stirring in his heart. She had told him that she came to London with one purpose—to make Michael regret what he had done to her. She hadn't been secretive about her desire for revenge when she first met him again at the masquerade.

What if she had never given up on her pursuit?

He squeezed his eyes closed, banishing his concerns. They scratched at his heart, filling him with dread like he had never known before. His lungs refused to expand. His head was light.

What if this had been her intention all along? What if she had become close to his family, pretending to forgive him for the ruin he had caused her, pretending to love him —only to add to her ruse? It would have been a masterful plan, and one executed flawlessly. Michael's heart pounded so hard it hurt. She *had* been very interested in the painting. She had wanted to come see it. What if she had only come to his studio the day before in order to discover where he kept it hidden? What if their kiss had also been part of her trick?

That last thought hurt the most. A sense of betrayal wrapped its fingers around his neck, squeezing and shooting pain through every inch of his body.

He stopped himself. The words *what* and *if* were dangerous together. They would leave him spiraling into madness if he let them. There were many other explanations that were more reasonable than the horrific ones that played out in his head. There had also been the man that had been in his studio the day before, who had seen them come out from the closet. Patience had told that man about the hidden compartment. Could that man have used the information to steal the painting? The idea sent a thread of relief across his shoulders.

After thinking of a few other possible explanations, Michael managed to expel his suspicions of Patience from his mind, until a witness came forward that afternoon, stating that he had seen the thief fleeing from the scene with Michael's paintings. Another witness stated the same thing.

The thief hadn't been a man at all.

It had been a dark-haired woman wearing a blue pelisse with three brass buttons down the back.

Just a few minutes before Patience planned to leave Mary's house to visit the Cavinders, a knock sounded on her door. She was grateful for the distraction. Her nerves had been jumping and twitching all day at the thought of seeing Michael again. She had almost convinced herself to stay home with Mary, but she had finally gathered the courage to put on her gloves and bonnet and prepare to leave.

She needed to speak to Michael and acknowledge what had happened in the closet and what it meant. She also needed to discover why he had kept the portrait of her as a monster all this time. It had been bothering her ever since she had seen it sitting on that easel, hastily hidden behind a sheet. What if he planned to display it in the exhibition again the next spring? It had earned him so many clients after all. Her stomach tied itself in knots. Would he really betray her like that?

She thought of his kind, gentle eyes and the ardent way he had held her and kissed her the day before. How could he be capable of something so wicked? He did not want to hurt her. There was not a single particle of malice in his entire body, she was sure of it. There must have been a different explanation.

With her thoughts in a distant place, she finally wandered to the door of her bedchamber to discover who had come knocking.

Mary stood in the doorframe. Her ash-brown curls sat high atop her head and her brown eyes blinked up at Patience.

"Good day, Mary." Patience smiled, surprised to find a mischievous grin on her cousin's lips. "What is the matter?"

"There is a man who has come calling for you," Mary said. "A Mr. Cavinder. Why did you not tell me that these Cavinders you visit so often have such a handsome son?"

A breath lodged in Patience's throat. Giddy elation swept over her body, and she nearly spun in a circle where she stood. Had he come to propose? He had never called upon her at Mary's house before. She smoothed her hands over her skirt, straightening her posture. Had Mary asked her a question? She could hardly remember.

Her feet carried her down the stairs and straight to the drawing room where Michael awaited her. She made it two steps into the room before she stopped, frowning.

There was something wrong about Michael's expression. His eyes were heavy, his mouth firm. His entire disposition was unrecognizable as he stared at her from across the room. He watched her with apprehension and dread, as if she might break him to pieces at any moment. He lowered a bow in greeting, far from the friendly gestures she had seen from him recently.

"Michael?" Patience took a step forward, her smile faltering. "What a surprise. I-I was just leaving to your house for tea." Her voice fell. Why was he staring at her like that? It was not a good stare, not the sort that made her stomach flutter. It was one that made her heart pound with dread.

His eyes were vulnerable, his arms folded. His features were all concentration as he studied her face as if he were trying to solve a puzzle.

"What is the matter?" she blurted, crossing her own arms. She was suddenly self-conscious. When he didn't answer for several seconds, she walked forward, stopping just a few feet in front of him. She searched his face, her worry expanding.

"I know what you did, Patience, but I want to know why." His voice was hoarse and broken.

She stepped back, scowling. "What do you mean?"

He rubbed one hand across his brow, shaking his head. "First, tell me where you put the painting. If you return it to me now, I will not hold you responsible. You may leave without punishment of any kind, I promise."

Patience's brow furrowed. "What on earth are you speaking of? What painting?"

Michael groaned. "Orpheus and Eurydice." His eyes flashed with hurt. "Stop pretending. You have done enough of that. I know you stole it. Two witnesses have now confirmed that the thief was you."

She shook her head. Her stomach twisted, and she felt suddenly ill. "Your painting was stolen? When?"

Vexation crossed his features. "Last night."

How could he blame her? Did he not realize how she had changed over the last several months? She remembered the monstrous painting that still sat on his easel. Perhaps that was how he had seen her all along—perhaps his opinion had never actually changed. Her heart cracked. "Well, the witnesses are wrong." A flash of anger shuddered over her body. "It was not me."

Michael studied her face for a long moment, his own heartbreak evident behind his eyes. He seemed resolved not to believe her. "If this is part of your revenge, then of course you wouldn't tell me." His voice was defensive and hard. "Why would you tell me the truth now when you have been lying to me all this time? You have betrayed my trust and my heart." His voice cracked, and he swallowed hard.

His words fell in the space between them, floating down like dead autumn leaves.

Betrayal sank through her bones. How could Michael

not trust her? Her own defenses rose, guarding her heart like an army. They had done it before, so they knew the procedure. Her pain was replaced with anger, and she threw her own accusation at him. "I saw *The Monstrous Debutante* on your easel yesterday. You had hidden it behind a sheet in an obvious attempt to keep me from seeing it." She swallowed hard, letting her anger prevail. "Do you plan to display it at the next exhibition again? You might benefit from its popularity a second time."

Michael's voice was quiet but firm. "No. I was using it as a reference for the new portrait I was painting for you."

Her heart stung. "And why should I believe you if you do not believe me?"

"How could two witnesses be mistaken?" Michael let out a long sigh, running a hand over his hair. He wouldn't look at her. "I did not come here to argue with you, Patience. I came to try to understand."

"Then understand me when I say that I didn't steal your painting," she said, her voice harsh. The walls around her heart creaked with the weight of the tempest that crashed against them.

Michael met her gaze, his own filled with grief. He studied her for a long moment, and when he spoke, his voice was broken. "You have fooled me once before. I only regret that I was not wise enough to avoid it a second time."

His words snapped like a whip, despite how quiet and broken they were. She was proud of herself for waiting to cry until after he exited the room. Her defenses came crashing down, shattering on the floor. If there was no way to prove her innocence, then how would he ever believe her? He wouldn't listen. He seemed to have boarded up the space around his own heart, much like she had done after Hattie had betrayed her. She had finally learned how to tear down her own walls, but she didn't know how to tear down Michael's.

If the piece he had been working on for months had just been stolen, then his emotions had already been fragile. She wiped at the tears on her cheeks. He had needed someone to blame, and all the signs had pointed to her. But how on earth had two witnesses claimed to have seen Patience walking away with the painting? It simply didn't make sense. Was there someone who had framed her? Someone who wished to ruin her life? If that was their wish, then they had succeeded.

She had never known ruin like this.

CHAPTER TWENTY-THREE

A letter sat on Patience's writing desk when she walked back to her bedchamber. The folded square looked unfamiliar to her, forlorn and strange. She couldn't remember the last time she had received a letter.

She wiped the tears from her cheeks, biting her lip to keep from sobbing again. Michael's words in the drawing room still sent pain radiating through her chest with every movement she made. She approached the letter with careful steps. It had come from Briarwood.

Her fingers shook as she unfolded the foolscap. Written in her father's hand was a brief message. She could practically hear his unyielding voice in the back of her mind as she read the words.

Patience,

Mary has written to me to inquire after how long you will

be staying in London. She has requested that you be returned to Briarwood at our earliest convenience. Thankfully, it happens that I planned to write to you of a different matter that should call you back to Inglesbatch as soon as possible. The Viscount of Fordwich has expressed his interest in you. He happened upon your portrait at the Royal Academy and it met his attentions with a surprising fascination. He is already aware of your broken engagement with Lord Clitheroe, yet he still wishes to meet you. I believe it is his eccentric nature which causes him to find something greater than disgust in these dreadful circumstances which surround your reputation. A connection with him would benefit our family greatly. We expect your arrival soon.

He signed the letter as he would any business correspondence, without any mention of the fact that he was her father. Without any indication of affection. Patience stared at the words written in his narrow, tilted hand. Mary and John didn't want her. Michael didn't want her. And her family only wanted her when she could be of service to them.

She thrust the letter down to her desk with disgust, but her eyes remained fixed on it.

She couldn't take it lightly. An offer from a *viscount*, after all that her reputation had suffered, would be unheard of. To marry this man, whoever he was, would at least secure a future of comfort for herself. She knew in her bones she would not be happy with him, but she could at least know that she wouldn't end up abandoned and alone. Her heart ached as she thought again of Michael. If she rushed away now, it would only affirm his suspicions of her. But what choice did she have? Mary and John were eager to have her leave, and she had no where else to go.

She slid the letter to the corner of her desk, hardly able to look at it. Her vision blurred with fresh tears. Michael had made his opinion of her clear. Betrayal and hurt clutched her chest so hard she couldn't breathe. If she left, it would come as a relief to him. He wouldn't even miss her.

But she would miss him. She would miss his reassuring smiles and contagious laughter, the feeling of his arms around her and the endless expressions of his eyebrows. She would miss his kindness, his deep thoughts and creative words. She would miss Mrs. Cavinder and her gentle good-ness, Emma and Isabel with their infectious love for life and new experiences.

Among it all, she would miss her heart. Because that broken, bitter thing they had all helped her heal would remain here in London with them.

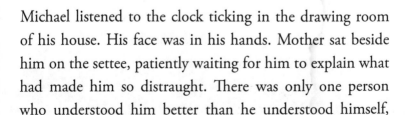

Michael listened to the clock ticking in the drawing room of his house. His face was in his hands. Mother sat beside him on the settee, patiently waiting for him to explain what had made him so distraught. There was only one person who understood him better than he understood himself, and that was Mother. She would know what to say to comfort him. Perhaps she could stop the pain and unease from festering in his heart.

He wanted to believe Patience. With every fiber of his being he wanted to believe her. Was it weakness that made him so eager to trust her? If he kept her close, how many more times would she trick him? The confusion in her eyes that day still haunted him, even as he sat in his drawing room hours later. Either he was mistaken, and somehow the two witnesses were wrong, or she was an incredible actress.

He groaned, sitting up to face Mother's concerned glance. His throat tightened with emotion as she wrapped her arm around his shoulders. Her brow knit together in worry. "What has happened?"

He had likely appeared just as distressed the year before when he had been preparing to tell her that they could no longer afford his father's studio. Mother seemed prepared to hear similar news again.

"The painting I have been working on for months…the one I planned to display at the next exhibition was stolen this morning."

Mother gave a quiet gasp, shaking her head. "Were you harmed?" Her eyes flitted over him with concern.

Harm had been done, but it wasn't anything she would be able to see. The pain he felt was like a knife deep in his chest, stabbing and twisting without mercy.

"Who would do such a thing?" Mother asked. "Oh,

Michael. I know how much time you spent on that painting."

He shook his head, closing his eyes against the ache in his forehead. "That is not what troubles me the most. Yes, having another painting displayed at the exhibition would have benefitted us greatly, but you haven't heard the worst of it."

Mother's eyes rounded, and she sat back against the cushions. "Tell me." She braced herself on the armrest of the couch, her hand curving over the edge to grip the upholstery.

"Two witnesses who were passing by my studio this morning described the thief. Their descriptions matched Patience." A fresh pang of grief struck him. "It made sense. She came to London to seek revenge on me, but I was foolish enough to think she had changed. I was even foolish enough to fall in love with her." His voice broke and he bit the inside of his cheek.

Mother was shaking her head. "No, Michael, you must be mistaken. Patience would never do something so wicked. She has changed, and you know it. It is obvious to me that she loves you too."

He turned toward his mother, heart thudding. She was much wiser than him. She always had been. If she thought Patience truly loved him, then how could it not be true? Frustration mingled with his confusion. But how could the other evidence be explained? "Patience was the only person who knew where I kept that painting hidden," Michael said.

"That is not enough to condemn her," Mother said. "Your shop has many windows. Any person passing by undetected could have peered inside and watched you hide the painting at the end of any given day."

Michael nodded. "That is true. But what of the witnesses? I spoke to both individually," he said. "Both said that they saw a dark-haired woman wearing a blue pelisse. The blue pelisse was described to be exquisitely detailed, with three brass buttons down the back, symmetrical pleating, and a tall collar. Patience has worn that very thing more times than I can recall."

Mother threw a hand over her mouth. She leapt from the settee, turning to face him.

He jerked back against the cushions, shocked by Mother's sudden movements. She paced in front of him, shaking her head. "I hope you have not already accused Patience of stealing the painting."

He was silent for a long moment.

"Michael." Mother stopped, jaw hanging loose. She was usually the picture of composure, but something in his last words had unraveled her. "Did you?" She scolded him with her gaze.

"I wanted an explanation," he said. "So I did speak with her, but she denied that she stole the painting."

Mother closed her eyes with a sigh. "She denied it because she did *not* steal it."

He frowned as his pulse picked up speed. "How do you know?"

With slow steps, Mother returned to her seat beside

him on the settee. She placed one hand on his knee. "Do you remember the day you returned home and she sat near the fire with me? She ran from the room because she was ashamed of the scars on her arm."

Michael nodded.

"Did you ever wonder why her arms were uncovered that day?"

As he thought back to that moment, he realized he had never questioned it. He had been too concerned with Patience's tears to wonder why.

He shook his head.

"I found her on the front steps, arms bare, shivering, but she hesitated to come inside. She was distressed about something. She told me that she had given her pelisse to a cold, poor woman in the street. In answer to her kindness, that woman had then stolen Patience's reticule."

Realization crashed over him.

"Patience does not even have that blue pelisse anymore." Mother's words came faster. "The woman she gave it to had already proven to be a thief once before. I am entirely certain that it was she who stole your painting, not Patience."

He covered his face with his hands, regret spiraling through his stomach. What had he done? His accusations had been harsh, a result of his broken heart. He had no excuse for it. His pride had hardened him, making him unwilling to listen and risk making a fool of himself by trusting her. Amid it all, relief still flooded his soul. Patience hadn't betrayed him.

But now he had betrayed her. He was like Orpheus, unwilling to trust that Patience could change from darkness to light. He had given up too soon, and now he might have lost her forever. He didn't care about the painting. That thief could do with it what she wished. All he wanted was to take back the things he had said to Patience.

He groaned into his palms. "What shall I do now?"

"Apologize to her at once." Mother patted his knee with force. "Do not leave her with her confusion a moment longer. Go."

He stood, thanking Mother with his eyes before leaving the room. She wouldn't have wanted him to linger with any words of gratitude. He had a grand apology to make, and no matter how carefully he planned his words, there was no way of knowing if it would be enough.

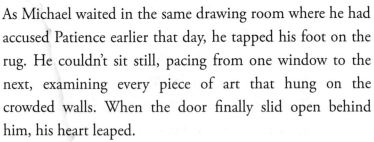

As Michael waited in the same drawing room where he had accused Patience earlier that day, he tapped his foot on the rug. He couldn't sit still, pacing from one window to the next, examining every piece of art that hung on the crowded walls. When the door finally slid open behind him, his heart leaped.

Patience stood in the doorway, chin held high. Her eyes were fierce, as if daring him to accuse her again. Guilt fisted its hands around his throat. He couldn't speak. How could he have doubted her for one moment? As he looked at her now, he saw the glistening lines of dried tears on her cheeks. The fierce glare she gave him faltered as he walked toward her.

"Patience, I am so sorry." He shook his head as he took her hands in his. She looked down, her jaw hanging loose with surprise. "I know now that you didn't steal the painting. I-I was rash and unkind. I should have listened to you, but I was afraid to make a fool of myself by trusting you a second time." He let out a sigh, searching her face. "My mother told me how you gave away your blue pelisse. The woman the witnesses saw was wearing it. That was the greatest source of my confusion. I wanted to believe you, and I should have." He could think of nothing more to say, nothing that would not be repetitive. "I'm sorry. I truly am."

Patience didn't say a word, staring up at him with a furrowed brow. Her lips were solemn. "I was just packing my trunk, you know."

His heart fell. "Where are you going?"

She was silent for a long moment, looking down at their hands. "My father invited me home. There is a viscount he would like me to meet."

A surge of dread tore through Michael's chest. He had already behaved like Orpheus once, so he ought not to allow her to venture back to Hades, or, in this situation, her father, Lord Ryecombe. "You mustn't go back to them, Patience. I have seen how unhappy it made you."

She pressed her lips together. "I know." Her eyes fluttered up to his, still hesitant. "But for a moment I was also truly unhappy *here*."

He knew the precise moment she was referring to. His heart broke all over again.

"I thought you would never speak to me again." A tear hovered on the edge of her eyelid. She blinked hard. "You have caused me several hours of stress, you know."

"I know." Michael moved without thinking, wrapping his arms around her and pulling her into his chest. She was stiff at first, but then she melted against him. He could feel her trembling. He rested his chin on top of her head. "How many times will I ruin you before I learn my lesson?"

A quiet laugh passed through her body, vibrating against him. It was his favorite sound in the entire world.

He could easily envision his future with Patience, and he yearned for it so much it physically ached. They had already learned to forgive one another, many times over, and they would likely have to continue doing so throughout their entire lives. That was what happened when two imperfect people happened to be such a perfect match.

"I knew I never should have given that horrible woman my pelisse," she said. "Now she has my favorite item of clothing, my reticule, *and* your painting. Not only that, but she has framed me for the crime in the process." She sniffed, looking up at him. "Is there justice for people like her? Like my sister Hattie? Why should they be allowed to carry on with their lives without any punishment?"

Michael brushed a curl from her forehead. "There is a reason revenge is so tempting. It would offer temporary relief to see their deeds punished, but in the end, the hatred and anger is still yours to carry. This thief, as well as your sister, may do as they wish. Your happiness is independent of their actions."

Patience gazed up at him. Her hazel eyes were still slightly hesitant, but she no longer glared at him. He would consider that a small victory. In that moment, he was reminded that his happiness was entirely dependent on her staying in London. "Do you still plan to leave?" He held his breath as he awaited her answer. He was fully prepared to beg her to stay if he had to.

A flash of uncertainty crossed her features. "I-I don't know."

He looked down at her soft pink lips. If he kissed her again would that help her decision? The temptation set his heart thudding against his ribs. "Who is this viscount? Are you interested in marrying him?" He tried his best to keep the envy from his voice, but it still managed to slip through.

"My cousin and her husband do not want me here." Patience looked down at the floor, her voice growing quieter. "I-I fear I no longer have another choice but to return to Briarwood."

He wanted to reassure her that she *did* have a choice. She could stay in London with him, as his wife, and move to his townhouse with his family. His throat was dry, his hands weak as he swiped a tear from the side of her face. He would have proposed to her right then, but he had a much better plan. He needed just a little time to prepare. "Come join my family for dinner tomorrow," he said.

Her brow furrowed. "What difference will that make?"

"That will depend on your answer." He smiled, pressing a soft kiss to her forehead.

A lovely shade of pink flooded her cheeks. Her eyes shifted to his lips, and it took all his concentration not to kiss her properly on the mouth. "My answer?" Her voice was filled with confusion.

Michael shouldn't have taunted her so much, but he couldn't help it. He stepped away with great effort, backing toward the door.

"I will see you at dinner tomorrow evening."

A slight smile pulled on her cheeks, but it was hesitant, as if she were afraid to trust the hope he was giving her. He was afraid too, because it was still possible that she might not accept his proposal. She might have needed more time to forgive him for his accusations toward her. But he couldn't wait. He needed her to know without any doubt how much he loved her.

Just before he took his leave, he cast her one last smile. "And please do not run off and marry that viscount while I am away."

She shrugged one shoulder, her eyes locked on his. "I am a little impatient, you know."

He laughed, holding her gaze for a few seconds more before slipping out of the room.

CHAPTER TWENTY-FOUR

*I*t was impossible to stay angry with Michael, not when he had such obvious remorse and the eyes of a puppy.

Patience approached the doors of his townhouse with a deep breath. Her veins thrummed with excitement. The long chiffon sleeves of her gown did little to keep the cold air away from her skin, so she hurried inside the moment the door opened. During the time since Michael had called upon her to apologize, she had found it nearly impossible to focus on anything but her anticipation of that very evening.

To distract herself, she had written a letter to Hattie. It had taken her hours to draft, and another several hours to seal and post. In the letter, she had explained the feelings she had kept hidden for years. She explained how diminished Hattie had made her feel. It had come as a relief, a healing balm, to write those words. At the end of her letter, she had given Hattie the same piece of wisdom Michael had given her. People are not paintings. They exist for far more than to be looked at and admired.

Just before signing her name, Patience had expressed her forgiveness and wished Hattie well. She had even meant it. Deep in her bones, she hoped that her sister would find the sort of happiness Patience had tasted here in London with the Cavinders. She hoped Hattie would eventually feel remorse for her mistakes and that she would seek to mend them.

She had written a similar letter to Mama, and then she had written a reply to her father. She had told him that she would not be returning home because she would be marrying Mr. Cavinder.

She hoped Michael would not make her a liar.

As she walked into the entryhall, she glanced at the space all around her. There were more candles than usual, brightening the room in a warm glow. Michael's household did not have very many servants, but the few that did occupy the small house stood at attention, lining the wall by the stairs.

Was this a formal dinner? Each time Patience had dined with the Cavinders, they had treated her as they would a close family member, doing away with certain social rules and expectations when it came to dining. Tonight, the house held a different air. The evening was important, distinguishing itself from all the others. She was glad that she had worn her finest dress. The ivory satin and chiffon was elegant enough to match her surroundings.

Her thoughts came to a sudden halt when she caught sight of Michael.

Even at the theatre he had not looked so handsome and formal. She had grown accustomed to seeing him in his shirtsleeves and paint-streaked smock, with his hair falling messily over his brow. Tonight, however, he was dressed in black. His boots were shined, and he wore a snowy white cravat. Combined with his freshly shaven jaw, and hair combed away from his face, she could hardly breathe. Her heart shuddered when he smiled, his eyes drinking her in with just as much reverence and awe as she felt.

He strode forward, taking her hands when he reached her. He traced his thumb over her knuckles, lifting them to his lips. His eyes rose to meet hers. "My mother and sisters are waiting in the drawing room," he said. "But there is something I must show you first." His lips curled into a grin as he reached into his pocket. He withdrew a long, folded piece of fabric.

Patience stared at it with confusion before realizing what it was. "A blindfold?"

"Yes. It will add to the suspense." He brushed the hair away from her forehead, sending a string of shivers over her skin.

She cast him a suspicious look before he draped the fabric over her eyes, tying it behind her head. A giddy excitement rolled over her shoulders, making every muscle in her body tighten with anticipation. His hand slid around her upper arm, the other pressing against the small of her back as he guided her steps forward. "Where are you taking me?" Her voice was breathless, mingled with her laughter.

His voice came close to her ear. "If I told you, that would defeat the purpose of your blindfold."

Mounting the stairs was difficult without her vision, but she managed to obey Michael's instructions, safely reaching the top. Her cheeks ached from smiling when Michael finally stopped her, placing both hands on her shoulders.

"Keep your eyes closed when I remove the blindfold. Do you promise?"

"Yes."

He untied the knot on the back of her head, slipping the fabric away from her face. The abundance of candlelight filtered through her eyelids. "May I look yet?"

"Be patient." His voice carried a hint of teasing.

His footsteps trailed away and then returned to her side. She heard him draw a deep breath. "Open your eyes."

The candlelight intensified, and she blinked several times before gazing up at the wall in front of her. She gave a quiet gasp, pressing a hand to her chest. She whirled to face Michael, heart pounding. It was a new portrait of her in the size she had originally requested more than one year before.

"As I said before, this is the only reason I kept *The Monstrous Debutante*." Michael's voice broke the silence.

"Without you sitting in front of me, I needed something to reference as I completed this new one."

A surge of emotion gripped her throat, and she looked down at the floor. She shook her head, covering her mouth with one hand.

Michael tucked his fingers under her chin, cupping one side of her face. "Do you hate it?" His brow creased with concern.

Patience rubbed the space beneath her nose, shaking her head fast. She was so overcome, so helpless to her emotions, that she could hardly speak. Her voice was a garbled mess. "I love the portrait. I-I love all of it." She couldn't finish. It wasn't the portrait that had caused her tears, but the way it hung on the wall, directly beside Michael's portrait. On the other side of his hung the likenesses of his late father, his mother, Emma, and Isabel. Patience's own father had taken her portrait down from the gallery because she had not been good enough. She had not belonged. To think that the Cavinders would be her family now was too much to bear. She wasn't certain her heart could contain so much happiness at once.

Michael caught each of her tears as they fell from her eyes. "Hanging it here beside my own was a large assumption, but I also hoped it might persuade you to give me the answer I'm seeking." He cast her a glance that was uncharacteristically bashful. It melted her heart.

She sniffed, laughing.

His eyes searched hers, his lips curving in a smile as he held her face between his hands. The raw adoration in his gaze made her legs unstable. "I also wish to submit it for display at the exhibition, if you'll permit me. The entirety of London ought to see you like this. I wish for them to know you as I do. Beautiful." He pressed a kiss to her forehead. "Good." His lips trailed over the hollow of her temple. "Far from monstrous."

She sighed and tipped her chin upward.

"I love you, Patience." The declaration was simple, but it unfurled wings in her chest and made fresh tears spill down her cheeks.

"I love you, too."

Will you marry me?" he asked in a quiet voice.

She nodded, nudging her nose against his. "Yes."

A smile curled his lips just before they captured hers. This kiss wasn't the fire and desperation and uncertainty that their last kiss had been. This time it was peace, hope, and belonging that encircled her, squeezing tight and promising never to let go. She kissed him with the same fervor he displayed, grateful that their only spectators were a row of portraits on the wall. His insistent lips seared promises into her skin as he trailed kisses over her face and neck and back to her mouth again.

She wrapped her arms around Michael's shoulders at the same moment his arms surrounded her, pulling her impossibly closer. Her feet lifted off the ground as they spun together, laughing and kissing and daring to dream of the future that they would now share.

There was still a great deal Patience hadn't yet overcome, but she suspected that that was why the natural course of life was much longer than her twenty-one years. She couldn't even begin to imagine how much stronger and better she could still one day become. Because for the first time in her life, she was safe. She was wanted. Most important of all, she was loved.

OTHER BOOKS IN THE SONS OF SOMERSET MULTI-AUTHOR SERIES

Carving for Miss Coventry - Deborah M. Hathaway
The Stable Master's Son - Mindy Burbidge Strunk
An Agreeable Alliance - Kasey Stockton
The Highwayman's Letter - Martha Keyes

ABOUT THE AUTHOR

Ashtyn Newbold grew up with a love of stories. When she discovered chick flicks and Jane Austen books in high school, she learned she was a sucker for romantic ones. When not indulging in sweet romantic comedies and regency period novels (and cookies), she writes romantic stories of her own. Ashtyn also enjoys baking, singing, sewing, and anything that involves creativity and imagination.

Instagram: @ashtyn_newbold_author
  Facebook: @authorashtyn

Made in the USA
Las Vegas, NV
24 November 2021

35249153R00157